This World Between

Erotic Stories

This World Between

Erotic Stories

MONIQUE POIRIER

Circlet Press, Inc.

Cover art credits:
Night sky © Denis Belitskiy
Venetian Mask © Robyn Mackenzie

ISBN 978-1-61390-182-3 ebook
ISBN 978-1-61390-183-0 paperback

Circlet Press, Inc.
39 Hurlbut Street
Cambridge, MA 02138

www.circlet.com

Contents

Introduction

Desire is a fickle thing; what is it that makes a common spark ignite between two people when they meet? These are the stories of eight such meetings across eight very different worlds – worlds like and unlike our own. Worlds of the future, the past, worlds of magic and wonder. In each of them, a pair of people meet, and join, and tangle their lives around one another.

The challenge of writing short stories is seeing how much richness can be crammed into ten pages or less. Can I start with a single concept or image and, in the space of ten thousand words, build an entire world? Can I make the reader ask questions, then give them answers to those questions? Can create two characters who beguile the reader as much as they beguile one another?

These stories each began with a call, a suggestion of time and place made by the editor of an anthology in the making. Clockwork histories, time travelers, crushing dystopias, fate and fortune, angels and demons, fae creatures, fairytales, Lovecraftian nightmares... these were the starting blocks from which I raced away. These are the worlds that came to me, and the people who live and love in them.

My hope for you, reader, is that you'll enjoy exploring these worlds and meeting these characters as much as I enjoyed creating them.

Monique Poirier

September 2018

At the Crossroads

The brothel in The Gray City was reported to be the most extensive in all the world; a city in its own right. If I couldn't find what I needed here, then there was no hope left for me.

The Gray City stood at the crossroads between light and darkness, the last border of either, and the whole of it was considered neutral ground. That did not make it safe, by any means, but it was most probably the only place in all creation where an angel and a demon might meet without the obligation that one was to murder the other if possible. It was depraved, by the standards of light, but that was exactly what I needed now.

I'd known something of the inner workings of this labyrinth long before I'd arrived. The Seven Circles catered to every possible taste, from the richest nobles who walked along the pathways of the tower to the common street trash who wandered the twisting alleyways known colloquially as "the gut."

It was the gut that I stalked through now.

The price of admission to the gut was two alliance shillings, but the keeper of the gate had taken a glance at me and let me pass without comment. Perhaps he assumed that I was about official business—I seldom wore anything other than the uniform that marked me an Archon. Perhaps it was only that I was a winged man with a sword at the ready; only a half-blood, but most mortals took me for a proper angel. That made a startling number of them give me wide berth.

If I chose to ascend from the gut, I'd be charged again at every staircase and eventually at every door. This was the nastiest and most dangerous level of the complex, with twisting allies and tiny rooms that could be rented by the half hour. The whores that milled around at this level were those who hadn't the quality to make it to higher levels—or those who had fallen. The old, the maimed, the insane, the diseased. My entrance fee meant that any flesh that I found to my liking was mine for the taking—brute force wasn't discouraged, and no one, including other customers, was off-limits. There were guards here, but they cared only for the general peace and the interests of the house. They served to keep those who belonged in the gut from leaving it. The gut of The Seven Circles was as close to Hell as a mortal could find prior to death. I wouldn't have stayed here, among the beggars and thieves and human offal, were it not for the fact that I'd caught the scent I craved.

It was nearly a week since I'd run down a band of incubi on the border with my comrades and been bitten by more than one of them in the final battle. The venom was still coursing through me, slowly driving me mad. The ones who'd bitten me had taunted me with lavish offers of pleasure at the time, and it had been a feat of great will that I'd resisted such offers long enough for my comrades to extricate me through blood and steel.

My comrades, being wholly human, had little idea of what I could do to rid myself of the venom save finding a demon and slaking my lust upon it.

Six days the need had been made to build and fester. Now it was like a fire in my mind, burning away rational thought, widening my options until every person I glanced at became a considered object for my lust, and every whiff of sweat told me that they were useless. I could fuck a hundred mortals with incubus venom in my blood and still meet no satisfaction—I wasn't entirely sure how I'd come to that conclusion, but I knew it as rote fact in any case.

I'd caught the scent here—sweat and spice and that fiery twinge of rightness that I craved—the scent of a demon. I followed it ruthlessly, pushing aside any who were foolish enough to stand in my way in single-minded pursuit. My eyes darted in the direction that scent came from, searching the crowd. The stale wind shifted, and it came strong and sudden. I spun around a corner, and caught sight of my quarry.

Beautiful.

He sat in the shadow cast by the waist-high wall surrounding the courtyard, eyes closed, features drawn tightly in exhaustion. There were bands of iron at his wrists and throat, marked in sigils that I dimly knew. His head was shaven within a quarter-inch of his scalp. The same could be said of fully half the whores in the gut; it kept the lice at bay. What remained was dark, contrasting skin the color of dust. His clothes were in tatters, but seemed clean enough. His limbs were long and lean, his features too sharp to be called beautiful, but still compelling. A pair of curving horns, like those of a ram, rose from his hair in a stately arc. Here was the spawn of Hell, more achingly beautiful than any other creature I'd ever seen. More than that, his scent was *right*.

I was there in moments, gripping a handful of tattered clothing and pulling him close, feeling supple flesh beneath my fingers, breathing the scent of him. I hissed something, hardly aware of my own words. I was going to fuck him into oblivion.

———◉———

"FOUND YOU, FOUND YOU, found you!" the voice hissed as I was pulled onto my feet with absolutely no warning.

Fear flashed in my mind as I braced myself for a blow, but that didn't seem to be what this man had in mind. An arm snaked around my waist and pulled me close against the unyielding heat of another body, hand sliding down to cup and firmly hold my ass, preventing any retreat. Strong fingers splayed out against the knot of muscle at the base of my tail, and I instinctively curled it between my legs while his other arm slid across my shoulder, hand on the back of my head. He paused for a long moment, holding me in that fierce embrace.

Ah, so this was a customer.

He breathed against my neck as that hand ran over my shorn scalp, scenting me. Not the first to do so. It came with being a demon, something in my scent that mortals craved. His hand was very warm—fever warm—and trembling. He might have plague, though surely I'd have smelled that on him. He certainly didn't reek of death. In fact he smelled... nice. Really, very nice indeed. With the whole of his body against my own, I felt the hard length of him pressing into my belly. There was little doubt of what he wanted from me.

He backed away from the wall, one strong arm still locked around me so that I had no choice but to follow. He wasn't threatening me or asking my price or any of the other little rituals that were sacrosanct here. That was never a good sign. Wretched setback if he left me in some unfamiliar place and I had to work my way back to areas I knew, but there was no help for it now. I followed without a word, hoping that he would be done with me quickly.

There wasn't any warning; he pushed me and I fell backward onto a reasonably firm surface. Hay. He pinned me down, arms above my head, wrists held by his hands. He was very strong. The hard edges of a leather belt ran from his shoulder to his hip, and I knew damned well the feel of a baldric... he was wearing a sword. I didn't have time to analyze the situation further before his mouth was on mine.

My mind went gloriously blank, the intensity as hot, wet velvet invaded my mouth. No one ever kissed me. I went limp under the assault, my mind racing, my heart thundering in my own ears. Nobody kissed me. I was a slave of the Circles, less than a whore, and a demon besides. He'd found me in the gut, he had to know that I was worthless...

I returned that kiss with hunger, and he growled approval. I hadn't realized how starved I'd been for this kind of attention until he began a slow, even rhythm with his hips that made his hardness slide against my own hardening length. I whimpered into his mouth and tried to remember how long it had been since I'd last felt such heat tightening low in my belly. This kind of thing was for better sorts of people. Customers like this didn't linger in the gut. Customers like this didn't seek out demons.

He groaned, pulling away just enough to speak, the length of his body still pressing me down into the hay.

"Tell me I can have you," he panted, grinding his cock against mine, "need you so much. Need to fuck you. Tell me I can. Tell me," each pause punctuated by a thrust of his hips.

"Yes sir," I whispered in reply before I could let myself think about it.

It was the first time I'd said "yes" to someone here.

———◉———

I SHOULD AT LEAST HAVE dragged him into a decent room and laid out coin for a bed, but the demon's scent was maddening, his flesh warm and supple under my hands, and the nearest deserted alleyway looked inviting enough. Lucky happenstance that it was being used to store baled hay, or I might very well have taken him against the wall. I was barely mindful enough to dig the vial of oil from my belongings, slicking it over my fingers and probing deeply in hungering exploration for a few moments. The demon probably wasn't ready when I entered him.

It was as perfect as I'd known it would be, and my moan of pure animal pleasure as I sheathed myself within the demon's body rang loud against the alley walls. His flesh held me, tightened around me beautifully, as he threw his head back and gasped. There was a fine sheen of sweat on his brow, his eyebrows knitted together as if in concentration, his jaw set, his tail lashing wildly for a moment and then wrapping itself around my calf. I was hurting him. Evil of me. Evil had been visited upon me, and now he was suffering for it. I should have been able to control myself, incubus venom or no. Perhaps if I'd been a true angel and not a half-breed. Words were coming out of my mouth, and I was only half aware of them, a litany of apology as I slaked Hell-born lust in the demon's flesh.

———◉———

"I'M SORRY, I'M SO SORRY... next time, I promise... next time I'll make it so good for you..." he panted into my ear in counterpoint to thrusting hips. I closed my eyes and arched my head until the tips of my horns touched the firmness of hay behind me, my breath coming in quick gasps as I was filled again and again. He'd slicked the way with something, and the sensation was... novel. Nothing like the pain I was used to, and that spot inside me that turned my insides to liquid fire was touched intermittently. He was promising to make it good? This was as good as I'd ever known. It was clear that his first concern was finding his own release, that was to be expected of any customer, but there were so many prowling this place who could only be satisfied if they left their victims broken and bleeding in the wake of their pleasure. Why else seek whores in the gut? We were disposable.

He'd said next time. He intended for there to be a next time. If he meant to become one of my regulars, there would be more of this.

Wet heat descended on my neck, the velvet slickness of his tongue against my flesh. The sensation was alien, but rather nice, really. He kept at it, nipping and tonguing along my throat. There was a shifting of weight, a fumbling of the hands that gripped my wrists as he managed to free one without releasing me, then that free hand swept down my chest and belly. He found my cock and gripped it, and I answered with a cry, heat coiling low in my belly to match the pleasure that flashed through me when his cock touched that spot inside me. Oh, this was good—I couldn't help but move in return. I tried not to think about what it meant that I was enjoying this as well or better than ever I'd enjoyed such things in Hell.

He shuddered, and the teeth at my neck nipped sharply. His fingers dug into the flesh just above my hip, and for a moment I felt something brushing against my trapped arms... something breathtakingly soft and wholly unfamiliar. It was gone an instant later, but I'd felt it. He went still, his breath heaving, blanketing me with his heat and the slowly calming rhythm of his heart.

I could smell something sweet and spiced on his breath as he laid his face in the hollow of my throat, mingling with the scents of leather and sweat and something I couldn't put a name to; not at all unpleasant. So much nicer than anything I was used to. I found myself breathing deeply, drawing that scent in. There was an odd sensation running through me, so uncommon that it took me a moment to decipher. I wanted more than that. I knew that when he left me that I would stroke myself to release, dreaming of this.

But he didn't leave me. He rolled off, lying alongside me, and took hold of my cock again. I writhed helpless under his hand as he leaned in to claim my mouth again, stroking me in his fist while his tongue slid against my own. It was more perfect than anything I'd ever felt. He nipped and kissed his way along my jaw, working upward until he captured the lobe of my ear between his teeth. He bit me, a little jolt of pain running down my neck and I came undone, jerking against him, crying out in wonder as the purest of pleasure rolled through me.

For long moments I lay in shattered awe, with his arms casually twined around me and his breath against my neck, trying to understand why he should have done that. He'd brought me release.

If he'd asked it of me, I might have given him my soul.

Something soft again, this time blanketing the whole of my body. My hands were free now, and I tentatively brought one down to explore what was before me. It was soft, and smooth, and surpassingly warm.

It was a wing.

It was *his* wing.

"You're an angel," I whispered, all the air going out of me. I found myself unable to take another breath, running my fingers along the smooth feathers and feeling the power of muscle beneath.

"Half-blood, yes. I'll want you again soon. Very soon," he said, his breath was hot against my neck as he spoke and then suddenly cool as he inhaled deeply. "Several days, maybe longer. You'll come with me?"

"Days..." I said, mind racing. Such a long association; no one ever wanted me for more than a few hours, and seldom even that. Angels killed demons, and visited torment upon them in the name of righteousness. Absurd that I should be thinking on it at all; it wasn't even really a question. I'd go with him even if I refused—but he seemed to appreciate some pretense of consent on my part. If I humored him, I might be allowed certain liberties. I took a deep breath and dared to be bold.

"Will you feed me?" I asked softly. He didn't seem especially inclined to violence, but a slave speaking without express orders was a punishable offense. A demon daring to ask questions of an angel was as likely to be met with a flaming sword as an answer.

"Feed you? Yes. You'll come with me."

He pulled back from me, taking my hand and pulling me up with him. I heard the sound of rustling fabric, and then there was sudden movement around me; cloying warmth settled against my skin to match the weight that fell about my shoulders. It smelled richly of him, some garment of his that he'd seen fit to drape around me. It felt like an embrace.

My own clothes lay in shreds at our feet. I stooped to retrieve them, but he stopped me, taking my wrist and pulling me away. I hoped very much that he'd see fit to provide me with more before he discarded me. To be clothed in this place was certainly no assurance of safety, but to be naked utterly prevented it. His arm snaked around my waist again and drew me close, then a gust of air and the caress of smooth feathers at my back told me he had a wing curled around me as well.

I was tucked under an angel's wing.

The cloak he'd put on me was far warmer than my own clothes had been, even though I wore nothing beneath it, and my flesh sang in ap-

preciation of the improvement. There was no reason he should so much
as notice me, much less want me, and here I was tucked under his wing
and wearing his clothes. He was going to closet me away somewhere to
ravish at his leisure—for days, he'd said. He was an angel. It was his prerogative to do anything he liked with me, and no sane creature mortal
or otherwise would argue that.

A candlelight flicker of hope flared in me. If he kept me for days, I
might be able to snatch a few hours of sleep with him watching me. I
might be... safe. For a while. There was something pathetic about that,
that such a small thing should mean so much to me. That I'd trade my
body for it. I never said yes to anyone... but I'd said yes to him. I was
being tame for him even now, as I never was for anyone.

Because he'd been so careful with me. Because my skin still prickled
with the memory of his hands and mouth on me, of a kind of care that
no one ever spared for me. Demons did not deserve kindness.

I realized dimly that I was lost. I'd become very good at mapping
out this place in footsteps, but he didn't take any of the paths I knew.
He talked to several people. He was trying to find a room, but couldn't
find one that was to his liking. Eventually I heard the telltale jingle of
coins being passed from hand to hand.

"I'll do better later. I want you again now," he hissed into my ear. I
felt the closeness of walls and knew that we must be in a narrow hallway. A door opened, we went through, my foot brushed against something—and then his hand moved to the middle of my back and he
pushed me again, sending me stumbling forward. I braced myself for
the jarring pain of the floor and was pleasantly shocked to find myself
falling upon a yielding softness that invited me to press my face into it
and curl my fingers around it, mindlessly murmuring approval. It was
clean and soft and probably better than I deserved, certainly far better
than I was used to.

And then he shifted, and I knew that he was standing over me, and
that this luxury came at the price of my flesh. It wasn't a price I espe-

cially minded paying, not if it meant more of what he'd already been about. I turned over, leaning up on my elbows, and I waited for him to act.

I WAS A MONSTER. THE venom had made me such. No longer fit to carry the title of Archon, certainly, for what I'd just done and was about to do again. I couldn't bring myself to consider the real implications of this, not yet. I had a lithe body at my disposal, pliant and submissive and perhaps even willing. Mine. I could afford to be slower now; my earlier release had drained some of the tension from me and allowed a bit more coherent thought—but no less hunger. My clothes were an intolerable nuisance, and I quickly discarded them, looking down at my prize all the while.

He was terrified of me. Rightly so, as in any other situation I'd have been obliged to speed him back to Hell from whence he came—but at present I didn't like that fear, and my instincts sought to sooth it. He closed his eyes when I tried to meet his gaze, when I tried to tell him with my eyes what I couldn't gather the words to say.

I knelt, straddling him, lowering myself until I pressed full-length against him again, his racing heart beating against my chest, my arousal pressing into the soft flesh of his belly. His head tilted back slightly, exposing his throat, and his lips parted. The One help me, but he was beautiful. Was it only the venom that made me think so? There was corded tension in his muscles, quickness in his breathing, and the pounding of his heart. Fear.

I cupped his face in my hands and kissed him.

SOMETHING BROKE IN me when he kissed me again, because he moved so fluidly this time. There was so much more in it... before there had been hunger and need, and that was certainly in this kiss as well, but it was tempered with such reverence, such tenderness. An angel's kiss. I found myself wrapping my arms around his neck and running my hands down his back, fingers brushing against the joints where his wings met his shoulders. He seemed to like that, breath hitching for a moment before he moaned softly against my mouth. His hand snaked down, his cock pressed against my own and suddenly caught in his grip as he stroked both of us in his fist. It was more beautiful and intense and perfect than anything I'd ever felt, and in embarrassingly short order it had me coming with a cry, my tail wrapping itself around his leg again. He kept stroking, his hand almost painful in its intensity, until I felt his seed splash against my chest and belly, joining my own there. He blanketed me with his body, curling his arms under my back as he breathed a satisfied sigh against my neck.

WORTH IT.

It had been maddeningly frustrating to stay myself from simply sheathing myself in his flesh again, but it was very much worth it to have him purring against me, to have his arms casually twined around me, to have him sated, and smiling, and willing. This felt right, as nothing had in days.

"What's your name?" I asked, breathing in the salt of fresh sweat, my face against the hollow of his throat, lips brushing the band of iron that rested there. He gasped at the question, and stopped breathing altogether for several moments. Odd, and more than a little troubling.

Of course, I had unceremoniously fucked him without having asked his name to begin with.

"Loskeph, sir..." he breathed, barely audible.

"I'm Makhamir," I replied, studying the point of his jaw for a moment before placing a long, wet kiss. Tasting the salt of his skin, breathing his scent. I could grow drunk on this lovely demon's flesh.

The kiss was sweet, but it was the way he melted, going limp beneath me, that made a pang of heat shoot through me. It was the way he whimpered, speaking in the only language my venom-madness knew, telling me more about desire and fear and need and confusion than a thousand words could. It was magnificent. I raised my head to meet his eyes again, hoping that perhaps he'd let me do so this time. His eyes were opened wide, and for the first time I had a clear view of them. Gray-blue, the color of a thunderhead, almost white where the blackness of a pupil should have been.

"You're blind."

"Yes," he answered, his far-off eyes closing again.

"So that's why you're in the gut..."

"No," he answered, flinching as if he expected a blow. "Well... perhaps. I fell to the gut after my eyes were taken, but being a slave of the Circles is my punishment."

"Punishment?" I asked.

"Gross dereliction of my duties. Showing undue mercy to mortals. I released someone who didn't belong in Hell. I was banished for that." He breathed sharply, eyes pressed tightly shut. "They sold me here."

"And the keepers of the Circles took your sight?"

"The Gray City is far worse a place than Hell, half-angel. Demons are not nearly so inventive nor so demanding as mortals. My superiors knew that when they chose this punishment for me. Eventually I'll be broken enough to return to Hell, I suppose, and be properly contrite about my place there. It's what I was put here to learn. I strangled the first man who tried to take me. They gave me to a cleric who put my eyes out with blessed needles. I remember what it felt like, when I realized that I was blind and would remain so—my mind shattered. I was broken beyond all usefulness. I fell to the gut, and woke there because no one gave a damn even enough to feed me." He paused for a long moment, then opened his eyes before asking, "Why did you choose me?

You're an angel. You could have any whore from the tower for a song and a prayer. Why would you want me?"

I ran a finger along one of his curving horns, and he leaned fractionally against the touch. It made the corded tendons of his neck stand out in stark relief, and I found that I liked that quite a lot.

"I've been poisoned by the bite of an incubus. I need a demon. You suit me quite admirably."

His eyebrows rose, but he said nothing. I smiled a bit, gazing down at him. I'd been warned, as a child, that those who fell in sin spent eternity as the playthings of demons. I'd never considered having a demon as my plaything. I'd slain hundreds of demons for the glory of The One Who Is, but I'd never met one who'd writhe and moan and shiver at the simplest of caresses. I ran my fingers along the base of his tail, and it moved with all the speed of a viper to curl around my forearm as Loskeph flinched, eyes closed and teeth bared.

"Does it displease you to have it touched?" I asked, kissing his temple. The tension bled out of him, and his tail slowly uncurled.

"Those who touch it most often pull it..."

"That seems unpleasant," I said, electing instead to run my fingers carefully along the length of it from tufted tip to muscular base, venturing so far as to press my fingertip against the puckered hole beneath it. Loskeph drew his knees up at that, thighs readily parted, and a spike of desire crashed within me. Incubus venom was not something easily sated, it seemed.

But now I had a demon readily at hand, inviting me to do as I liked.

HE WAS CARESSING ME, apparently content with my supplication. His hands ran up along my sides, broad thumbs flicking over my nipples, and another cry died in the back of my throat. I was unused to such sensations, but I found that I craved them. Horrifying, that I'd finally found joy in my enslavement. Wonderful, that he should caress me, kiss me, touch me in ways that made me twitch and moan. It had been evil of him to remind me of how I'd come to this place. I'd withstood a thousand beatings with my pride intact, but a few well-placed caresses had me his willing whore. No, worse than that: whores could at least expect payment. A pair of tears escaped my eyes for the bitterness of it.

"You're weeping," he said, his voice clipped, almost a growl. Tears displeased him. It hurt that I already cared so much about displeasing him.

"I'm sorry," I choked, grasping for some answer that would please him, because as bitter as this was I wanted very much for it to go on. "You... you're so good to me."

And apparently that answer was perfectly acceptable, because his mouth was on mine again with the promise of tenderness and all thoughts of why this should hurt were gone from my mind.

He paused, rising up from me, and I heard the rustling of cloth and a warm, languid scent curled into the air, easily filling the small room. Slick fingers caressed me in the most intimate way, slipping into me with no resistance at all, finding that spot inside and toying with it. Oh, by all the power of The One who'd forsaken me, it felt good. Good enough to have my legs parted and my knees drawn up to grant him easier access, to have my toes curling in the sheets and my back arched. It hadn't been a lie. This was good enough to make me weep.

His fingers left me, and moments later he was inside me again, pressing inward in one long stroke. I tossed my head back into the impossible softness beneath me, overwhelmed by the sensation of being taken by one who meant it to be pleasurable. I wrapped my arms around him and pulled him close, bringing my hand tentatively upward along the back of his neck, nesting it in his hair. It was long, soft, and clean, a pretty luxury to touch. He purred approval, running his thumb in a quick circle around the head of my cock, making me buck and gasp appreciation.

All too quickly it was over—he was shuddering, his teeth pressing sharply into my shoulder, his seed spilling deep inside me. He lay still for a long moment, panting against my neck. I choked on another sob when he began moving again, fingertips moving down my chest and belly in prelude to soft kisses. I bit my lip against a scream when he took me into his mouth, and came much more quickly than I'd have liked because his mouth was a paradise beyond bearing. He drank me up, purring around me, running his hands in smooth patterns along the insides of my thighs. Eventually he moved up to lie alongside me, blanketing me with one enormous wing, humming tunelessly into my ear.

———————◦———————

THE VENOM-MADNESS WAS sated, for now. Swallowing his seed had quieted it more than anything thus far; I'd have to keep that in mind. I felt half drunk, and wholly exhausted, and more satisfied than I'd ever been in my life. The demon at my side panted, looking up at the ceiling with an expression of quiet ecstasy.

At least there was that much solace then, that he'd had been able to enjoy it. This probably wasn't something he'd have chosen, but we were linked now, he and I. I really had no idea how long incubus venom left one so affected; those who were bitten did not generally escape the incubus' ministrations thereafter. I'd been lucky, more than once. Lucky to escape before debasing myself among demons who'd happily drag me to Hell and lucky again to find another who'd moan and writhe beneath me.

"You wanted food?" I asked, trying to draw my mind from the thought before I found myself taking him again right here and now.

It was strange, watching emotion play out in blind eyes. But that was guarded hope, plain as day.

"I would like that very much."

"Well we should see to that, then," I said with a sigh, forcing myself, reluctantly, to rise. I cast a searching glance around the room for my clothes. They were scattered, and my shirt was torn. My cloak was beneath him. He had nothing to wear beneath it. Another thing I'd have to remedy.

"I want to buy you. Whom would I go to?"

Loskeph's face held a look of quiet disbelief, eyes wide and shining, his voice catching again.

"Buy me?"

"You've done me a great service," I said, offering him a hand and pulling him to his feet. "And I sincerely hope you'll continue to do so."

That announcement was met with a burst of hysterical laughter, and Loskeph's arms were thrown around my back. My wings moved to wrap around him, pulling him close against me. He was trembling.

"I'm a slave of the Circles. You're an angel. I'm fairly certain that you could walk out the front gate with me and no one would have the courage to stop you."

<hr/>

THE PASTRY WAS RICH as butter, melting on my tongue. The meat inside was juicy, the spices creating little explosions of flavor. I hadn't expected anything so mind-shatteringly good as this. Slaves were fed on gruel. Often enough I was waylaid from receiving my share of even that. I'd been too long without food if something so simple as a pastry could draw such a response from me. Maybe it was just that his presence seemed to sharpen all my senses.

Two promises made, both delivered. He'd made it good. He'd fed me.

Worse than that, I found that even walking through the market I felt *safe* with his hand in my hand and his wing at my back. Safe in a way that I hadn't felt for even a moment since awakening in the gut. Oh, this was trust, and it was going to get me killed.

He wanted to buy me... to be my master. The concept rang in my head like a bell, awakening things in me that I'd thought long dead. Old training of mine, things I'd been taught through pain and humiliation during my first days in the tower that I had learned very well. Things I'd fought, then, with fists and teeth.

He wanted me. Wanted to keep me. I was banished from Hell, and Heaven had never wanted me at all, but this angel wanted me. An angel that walked the earth, but an angel nonetheless. An angel with human blood, who might well be as capricious and cruel as any human, and had all the power of Heaven to back that wild abandon.

What did it mean for me that I was so happily submitting to his will?

This was probably a horrible setback in my progress toward earning my way back into Hell.

Even in Hell, no one had ever fucked me like that.

"It's hard to imagine you doing evil, Loskeph," he said to me, softly. Quite probable that he'd been watching me eat.

"I've done little enough of it," I answered. "I never was more than the least of the damned. Do you think banishment from Hell is meted out to those who are truly loyal? It's a thing done to half-breeds and mortal-lovers."

"But if you're not evil at heart, then what made you turn from the love of The One Who Is at all?"

I swallowed thickly, my mouth suddenly dry.

"It isn't a matter of goodness or of evil," I said with a derisive snort that was wholly beyond my station. Let him punish me for it, I didn't care. "It's a matter of obedience to The One Who Is. I do not belong to Him, and that He cannot tolerate. He is our maker as He is yours—demons are the children He does not love. How many demons have you killed without knowing that, angel? I've noticed that you carry a sword. What are you, in the wider world?"

"An Archon."

"A murderer of demons, then."

"I bring swift justice to those who do evil, mortal or otherwise," he corrected, and there was a tightness in his voice. It raised shrill panic in me, that he be displeased with me. I crushed that fear down with all the fortitude I could muster. I was after all a demon. I should not fear angels. Hate them yes, but not fear them. Not be supplicant to them.

Even when supplication meant gentle hands and burning kisses and fellowship and safety... when it meant all I'd ever wanted. I never had and never could belong to The One, but the core of me knew with terrifying certainty that I could belong to Makhamir.

"If we do evil, angel—and I will admit that most of us do—it is only that we learned at the feet of the master."

"I will not listen to you speak poorly of The One Who Is, demon."

He'd drawn very close to me; I could smell the heat rising from his skin.

"How will you stop me, angel?" I asked, bearing my teeth.

He lunged and crushed my mouth with his own.

———————— ◉ ————————

LOSKEPH NEVER FAILED to melt under my kisses. I took him from the pavilion where I'd bought the food and laid down coin for a room some ways above the gut, one with four strong walls and a locked door and an enormous feather bed, and I finished there what I'd started below.

He and I lived a tangle of sex and sleep and food and more sex for days.

More and more, as the days passed, we found ourselves lost in companionable conversation. I told him of my childhood in the holy city, my mother a temple virgin chosen to bear an angel's son, of my training as an Archon, and my adventures upon the roads of darkness and light. He told me of his life as a soldier of Hell, the wretched loneliness of it incomprehensible to me. Demons, it seemed, were not kind or loyal to one another. He'd known so much torment.

I woke on the sixth day and watched him sleep, sunlight poring over his face, and realized that I loved him as much as I loved any of The One's creations.

That was a problem that I did not know how to solve. I was obligated by honor to offer him his freedom for the service he'd done me, as soon as I was freed from the venom's curse. It was the least I could do to take him from this place and let him seek his fortune upon the road as a free man.

Loskeph stirred, sitting up, turning his head a bit as if to seek me out. I laid a hand on his shoulder and he turned to face me with a half-conscious smile.

"Do you know how long I'll be afflicted by venom?" I asked, twining my arms around his shoulders, pulling him back to rest against my chest.

"What do you mean?" he asked, leaning against me, tilting his head to offer me his throat.

"Not that I'm complaining, Loskeph," I said, placing a gentle kiss against the throat he'd so eagerly offered, "but for how many more days will I burn with the need to have you writhing beneath me? Surely you're growing tired of my constant demands."

Loskeph tilted his head a bit, as if I'd asked something very strange.

"You said it was an incubus that bit you, didn't you?" he asked.

"More than one, yes..."

"Then you'll need demon-lust for the rest of your life. It would hardly be an effective intoxicant for dragging immortals to Hell and keeping them there if it simply abated."

He might have punched me for the way the air went out of me then.

Damned. I was damned. The incubus who'd bitten me had damned me and cursed me with an insatiable need. I would go mad, or become a monster and be slain by my own comrades, or willingly consign myself to Hell for the amusement of demons. It was the sort of fate that befell

Archons, I'd always known that, but somehow I'd never truly expected to face it.

"It's my duty to patrol the roads..." I said, still breathless, not entirely certain of my words.

"Well if you're to keep on with that," Loskeph said archly, "you'd need a demon waiting for you in your bedroll each night. One who appreciates the awesome power of your righteous wrath and has no desire whatever to see you fall into Hell. I suppose it would help if he'd once been a soldier. It's my understanding that the roads to and from The Gray City are dangerous."

"You would come with me of your own free will?"

"Where else would I go, angel, and find greater satisfaction than in your bed? Put a collar and a leash on me if you must for your conscience, but I would follow you to the gates of Heaven or Hell or anywhere in between. I don't think you could prevent me."

I pulled him into a fevered kiss in reply, my wings closing around us and cocooning us within.

Complications of Heaven and Hell be damned; this world between the two was ours.

Concerning the Ars Mechanica

Doctor Kenneth Adlington sighed deeply, setting down his bag as he looked over the abandoned laboratory. He had until quite recently been on a sabbatical tour of the great clockworks of Germany, Belgium, Switzerland, and France. Upon hearing of his great uncle's illness, he'd returned immediately to Boston via overnight airship at no small cost, only to find that Uncle Benedict had died in the night. The physician told him that it had been an embolism of the brain, and that nothing could have been done.

Benedict Adlington had had seven children and twelve grandchildren, and none of them were in the least interested in the *Ars Mechanica*. It was thus to the surprise of absolutely no one that in his will he'd bequeathed the entire contents of his old laboratory to his great nephew Kenneth.

Kenneth was twenty-four years of age, a bachelor, and quite the most renowned mechanoscientist of his generation. Already since returning to Boston he'd been asked to give a lecture at Harvard University, an offer which he had not yet either accepted or declined. There was much on his mind, but he really did adore the *Ars Mechanica*, and if anything could soothe him after the recently upsetting turn of events it was throwing himself fully into his work.

The laboratory was located on the top floor of a recently-constructed building just off Beacon Street, overlooking the public gardens. Uncle Benedict hadn't used this laboratory for several years preceding his death, preferring the recently-added department of *Ars Mechanica* at Harvard University. It was startlingly quiet for a building nestled in the center of the city, and everything bore a fine layer of dust. Tools and projects lay haphazardly scattered about on steel tables of various heights. Roughly two-thirds of an automaton horse dominated one corner of the room, a careworn lab coat hanging from one of its tin ears. An antique Jacob's Ladder stood against the far wall, a clockwork dragonfly resting on one of its wires. A *Van de Graaff* generator stood dormant near the center of the room, various cords and wires leading to and from it.

Kenneth took out a notebook and began to make an exhaustive inventory.

It was well into afternoon and he'd gone through three notebooks when he discovered the laboratory's greatest treasure. Tucked into a corner underneath a canvas tarpaulin were a number of cheap pine crates, numbered in black paint in such a manner that it was clearly a set of related objects. His uncle being his uncle, a cursory exploration of the lab turned up a crowbar, with which he prised open the largest of the crates. The distinct scents of cedar and camphor assaulted his senses, and he sneezed before clearing the wood shavings away...To reveal what was very certainly the torso of a manlike automaton!

Kenneth's brow furrowed as he continued to open boxes. Uncle Benedict had very strictly eschewed crafting manlike automata and had in fact written a number of essays on the subject. He'd been of the opinion that automata best served man when they were unlike man—or rather that humanity itself wasn't fit to recreate humanity. Not when automata had in the last hundred years transformed from toys for the rich to a firm backbone of the mechanical revolution. Automata mined the coal that ran the great steamworks of Boston and New York, London, and Paris. Automaton horses were sturdier than their fleshy counterparts, requiring far less care and producing no excrement. Even children of relatively lesser means could afford tin pixies with photovoltaic wings that appeared to live on light and air—pretty, mindless things, with all the intelligence of butterflies.

Uncle had been of an older school of *Ars Mechanica*, more theoretical than utilitarian, that sought to mimic life with as much clarity and

vibrancy as possible. He'd been a true genius at the craft. He'd presented Kenneth with a clockwork terrier on his sixth birthday. That terrier, named Cogs, behaved so like a real dog that house guests were occasionally fooled until they petted him. It was that dog that had galva-
nized Kenneth's desire to study the *Ars Mechanica*. It wasn't enough to
mimic life: Uncle Benedict had been intent on mimicking intelligence.
When his clockwork dog barked, it did so for a reason. Automata with
minds were not much in favor except as curiosities, but a small portion
of mechanoscientists persisted in their study. Kenneth reveled in it.

Kenneth began to assemble the automaton as he uncovered the
pieces. The torso was in one box, the exquisitely crafted hands in another, the long and somewhat slender legs in another. It was quite a handsome piece of automata, as all of his uncle's creations were. True in pro-
portion, elegant in design. He felt a swelling admiration for the man
who'd designed such a wonder.

The head, when he found it in another carton, had him grinning
like a child fonding over his first tinker set. It was a smooth-fronted
hemisphere with the vaguest hint of a nose and deep caverns for eyes,
cast in something clearer than glass. Most likely some sort of morpho-
silicate crystal. Inside were the most intricate and lovely clockworks
and pneumatic cylinders, primarily of brass and copper. He lowered
his eyepiece and examined them at a closer magnification. Some of the
pieces were fine enough that they must have been laid with the small-
est of tweezers. Uncle had always had a watchmaker's hands; his colleagues marveled at it. The crystal was pierced throughout with hair-
thin strands of copper wire, the tips of which rested flush to the smooth
shell. Kenneth recognized a complex transparticular sensory apparatus
when he saw one. This automaton, when reconstructed, would have a
keen sense of touch. It was also possessed of a movable jaw of cast aluminum, and beyond it a tongue and throat composed of waxed leather
and similarly arrayed with minute sensors. There was a small wooden
box tucked into the carton alongside, and when Kenneth open it he

was somewhat startled to find eyes and teeth, along with a brass winding key. He smiled, gingerly removing an eye from the velvet that cradled it. It was blown glass, and possessed of such detail that it could well have served as a prosthetic—were it not for the inch-long brass spike protruding from the rear end of it. Curiously, he set one eye and then the other into their waiting sockets with care, leaning back to admire the effect. It was...unsettling. With eyes in place it was suddenly apparent just how like a skull the clockwork head was, and the eyes had a certain grim intelligence about them. They seemed to meet his gaze squarely and beg any number of questions. He removed the eyes again and put them safely back into their little casket before setting the head on the neck and attaching the myriad connections. Far easier to do such a thing without the unsettling feeling that the automaton was observing his progress.

The skin, neatly folded in the bottom of a crate that also contained a number of notebooks, was made of high-quality leather. It was supple and smooth, like a fine pair of gloves, and the interior side of it was coated with vulcanized rubber which had been well-powdered with talc to preserve its elasticity. The exterior side was the color of parchment and brushed to smooth softness that invited the touch of curious fingers. Upon further inspection, it was quite detailed in its craftsmanship. Fingers and toes each joined and textured, complete with fingernails of polished horn; the intricate shells of the ears. It was... most decidedly a male automaton. And very complete in that respect. Attention to anatomical detail had been very acute in that area, and Kenneth found himself more than a little embarrassed as he fitted the skin over the hard planes of the brass and steel framework, the bunched wires and brass plating in the all-too-lifelike semblance of muscle and bone. It required a level of intimacy that would have been wholly untoward if he weren't working on an automaton. He found himself quite inappropriately giddy in handling it thus. It was silly to be attributing feelings of modesty to something crafted from metal and glass and leather, but he found himself blushing in any case and after a few moments decided that, as there was no one around to chide him for it, he could damn well bend to propriety and dress the automaton in the lab coat.

Utter nakedness hidden only by a brief lab coat was hardly any better than nakedness unhidden.

Kenneth coughed into his fist and turned, fishing through the final box. He cleared the shavings away from the face, and suddenly found himself rather breathless.

It was as exquisitely crafted as the rest of the automaton, and Uncle must have hired an artist to accomplish it. The mouth was wide, with expressive lips, the cheeks sweeping and a bit severe as he fitted them over the crystal skull. But it was the mask the caught his attention.

A black velvet mask wrought with whorls of silver foil lay over the eyes, partly obscuring the face. It didn't seem to be removable, but rather crafted as a part of the face itself, lending a mysterious air to it. When he reluctantly placed the glass eyes and ivory teeth in their proper arrangement and fitted the face over them, he found that he had to blink several times and look away. The automaton was far too human in appearance and far too intelligent looking at that.

At the very bottom of the box that had contained the face, he found a wig of onyx-black curls, and he gingerly set it into place, hiding the last visible cogs and cylinders. The effect was quite complete; from a distance the automaton would very certainly pass for human. Kenneth took the little brass key and inserted it into the fitting at the nape of the automaton's neck with care. Taking a breath, he began to wind.

The exquisite machine began to slowly whir to life, the humming and clicking of a hundred thousand separate mechanisms blending together into an almost organic-sounding purr, like a finely tuned engine. Kenneth was startled when the automaton appeared to take breath, and then to cough. It adjusted the angle of its head slightly, and as Kenneth removed the key and pocketed it, the automaton staggered alarmingly. Instinct had him offering a steadying arm, and the automaton turned to face him. It moved with organic fluidity; none of the jarring, birdlike stops Kenneth was so used to observing in manlike automata.

The automaton met his gaze, and for the first time Kenneth saw that the gray eyes were lit from within, lending a wholly human sharpness and emotion. More than human.

"Who are you?" it asked, sounding genuinely startled and a bit anxious. "Where's Doctor Adlington?"

The voice was lovely. A smooth tenor, quite unexpected, and Kenneth found himself pausing just a moment too long to reflect upon it before answering. Intolerably rude. He coughed, looking slightly away from the automaton's arresting gaze.

"I'm sorry to have to inform you that your Doctor Adlington has passed on. Embolism of the brain. My name is Doctor Kenneth Adlington. Doctor Benedict Adlington was my great uncle," Kenneth said quickly. "I'm sorry."

"He's... gone, then?" The automaton said, its voice a bit distant. It, or rather he, was looking over the assortment of crates. "Have I been disassembled?"

"I'm afraid you have, until just now. It would appear that you've been so for quite some time." Kenneth answered, and only afterward considered how remarkable it was that the automaton showed such understanding of the situation and such curiosity.

"Gone...What is the date today?"

"It's November twelfth."

"Of what year?" The automaton clarified, sounding a bit impatient.

"1896."

The automaton's face was utterly blank, its eyes darting back and forth on a small patch of floor between their feet.

"Something's gone wrong. It... I wasn't. I... It was 1868..." he stammered, breath halting entirely. Unnerving, that.

"That could explain why I know nothing of you. You've been in those crates since before I was born. I'm dreadfully sorry."

The automaton looked back up at him suddenly, locking him in a piercing gaze.

"Do you own me now?"

"Excuse me?"

"Do you own me? You're a mechanoscientist, aren't you? You must be, you rebuilt me and no mere technician could do that. I'm quite a delicate piece of machinery, you understand. If Doctor Adlington isn't able to attend to my keeping someone else of skill will have to... Please understand that, Doctor, if you intend to sell me."

"Oh. Oh! You needn't worry about that. De Vaucanson's Act of 1877: 'All beings crafted by mankind must be treated, in respect to the law, with all the grace and dignity afforded to their God-crafted counterparts with consideration to their unique capacities.' As slavery has been abolished in the Empire since 1833 and in America since 1865, I can assure that no one owns you. I take it my late uncle hadn't seen to your citizenship?"

The automaton began breathing again.

"At the time it wasn't possible..."

Of course, I'm sorry. Well, that's something that will have to be seen to with haste. Tomorrow morning, I should think, we'll be able to get you registered with City Hall. There will be a written examination, but I don't expect you should have any trouble with that. You seem to be quite the most intelligent automaton I've ever had the chance to encounter. Why uncle would have relegated you to storage is quite unfathomable..."

The automaton closed his eyes briefly, a small smile playing at his lips.

"I thank you very much, Doctor."

"Please, call me Kenneth. There are few enough people who address me as anything other than Doctor Adlington these days, and that would simply be confusing given the circumstances. What's your name?"

"Hider."

"Excuse me?"

"After Oktav Haider, father of the reciprocating swashgyro?"

"Oh. Haider. Fine name... If I may ask, why is it that you're wearing a mask?"

He raised a hand, slender fingers touching the edge of the mask in an apparent show of self-consciousness, averting his eyes.

"Doctor Adlington said that it made me more human... If it makes any sense... I look more human when I look less human? He said that he could never quite get the eyes right. That my facial expressions were quite often all wrong and... uncanny. I don't smile well, I'm afraid." He paused for a long moment, then asked suddenly, "Do you dislike it?"

"No, not at all. I was merely curious. I'm sorry if I've offended you..."

"No, no, it's nothing like that. I worry. People have had any number of reactions to me, you see. Automata can be rather off-putting. But you're a mechanoscientist, you'd... understand that."

"I believe I do, yes. Well, we're beginning to lose the light, I'm afraid," Kenneth said, observing the deep golden cast of the sunlight splashed on the far wall. "No one's been by to refill the gas in these lamps in years."

"Oh..." Haider said, suddenly crestfallen. "You'll be going then?"

You'll be coming with me. I wouldn't leave you here, certainly."

He smiled wanly, tilting his head a bit, then looked down to regard himself.

"I've seldom left the laboratory. I fear I'm not dressed suitably. I would shock train passengers."

"That's alright," Kenneth replied with a grin. "I've got a motorcar."

———————◉———————

HAIDER WAS OUT OF HIS depth. Twenty-eight years had changed the world, and he watched it intently from the smoked-glass window of Kenneth's motorcar. The streets were lit with gas lamps, and people swarmed through them on foot and in all manner of mechanical contraptions: automaton horses with sleek aluminum skins; gyrocars on their enormous toothed wheels. He'd been shown schematics of such things, but when last he'd been aware they hadn't been a reality. When last he'd been aware...

———————◆———————

"OH, DMITRI... THAT'S very nice," Haider gasped, his fingernails biting into the wood of the table's edge. He had to be mindful and not chip his fingernails. They were very expensive and they wouldn't grow back like a man's would...

But Dmitri was so terribly clever with his mouth! He purred at Haider's compliment, and Haider shook, hands moving of their own volition to nest in Dmitri's hair—so pale a blond that it was nearly white, longer than was fashionable among Bostonian youth. Dmitri's hair was so pretty... One wasn't supposed to use that term with young men. Women were pretty and men handsome. Either could be beautiful in an objective sense. People called Haider beautiful quite frequently... Dmitri's hand crept along his thigh and that broad, warm palm was suddenly cupping and very gently squeezing his balls and he found himself quite unable to draw another breath. That was alright, as his breathing was purely aesthetic, but an interesting thing to note. Dmitri pulled back, lips just barely ghosting at the tip of Haider's manhood, and looked up at him with ice-blue eyes.

"Can I haff you?" he asked, the warmth of his breath an arresting sensation on Haider's mouth-slicked skin. He could feel each and every filament of his copper nerves crackling with electricity.

"Oh yes please," he breathed, allowing Dmitri to turn him, obligingly leaning over the table and standing with legs apart, as Dmitri had instructed before. He had a vague idea that Dmitri's evening lessons were untoward somehow, as he only arranged them when the lab was otherwise

*deserted and certain to remain so. None of Haider's other lessons had con-
tained any information at all about this sort of thing. But Dmitri was such
a very obliging teacher when the mood struck him. There was a short pause
as Dmitri liberally applied oil from a nearby flask to his straining manhood, and Haider looked on appreciatively. Dmitri's anatomy was somewhat larger than his own, though that was only to be expected as Dmitri
himself was rather a large man. Haider hadn't seen enough men in a state
of undress to make valid comparisons, really. The anatomy texts he was allowed certainly didn't show men in such a state of arousal, and when he
posed questions on the subject to Doctor Adlington the man simply turned
red and changed the subject.*

*Dmitri ran his hands along Haider's flanks, pausing at his hips, his
grip firm and demanding. His hand took an abrupt downward sweep,
and Haider let out a small noise of appreciation as it closed around his
aching length, a callused thumb running over the head, spreading slick
wetness there. He wanted to be louder, but Dmitri told him that they
mustn't be. He still found himself moaning in earnest when that
hand—broad, hot, slick—continued to caress him as Dmitri drove into
his body in one smooth stroke. He was on the brink of senselessness, unable
to comprehend such pleasure, totally given way to the sensations. Dmitri
gripped him tightly, whispering meaningless words into his ear, murmuring frantically in what Haider thought must be Russian. He gasped, cold
air shocking on Haider's sweat-slick skin, and when Dmitri spilled his seed
deep within him something in Haider's perceptions shattered apart, white
light and an odd dissolution and, oh, it was a finer thing than he'd ever
known...*

And then Doctor Adlington was shouting...

———◉———

THE MOTORCAR STOPPED, bringing Haider's thoughts abruptly
back to the present. He had no way of knowing what had happened
after that. Doctor Adlington had instructed him to sleep with the ex-

planation that he had to be thoroughly examined to determine if any damage had been done. His protests that Dmitri hadn't done anything unpleasant to him were silenced. He'd awoken again to Kenneth's curious gaze. Twenty-eight years. Doctor Adlington had thought his infraction on propriety severe enough that he'd put him away in his cartons and hadn't deigned to ever take him out again. Haider found his hands shaking a bit, trying not to dwell on that.

"Do you have any idea what you'd like to do concerning accommodations? You can certainly stay at my flat for as long as you'd like, but I'm afraid I don't have a spare bedroom to make up for you." Kenneth said, fitting a key into the front door lock and then holding the door obligingly.

"That's quite alright," Haider replied. "I don't sleep, in most circumstances. I rather prefer not to, actually. I only sleep if I'm not kept wound properly... You have the key, don't you?"

"Yes, in my pocket. Why is it that your winding mechanism is at the back of your neck? Rather a dreadfully hard place for you to reach, isn't it? Difficult for you to wind yourself, if need be?"

"I do believe that's the reason for the design, Doctor," Haider said, closing the door behind them.

"Hmm. And please, it's Kenneth! If you address me as Doctor, I'm apt to start thinking of you as one of my undergraduate associates–you do look terribly young, you know. Was that a deliberate part of your design, or incidental?"

"I... don't know. Doctor Adlington never talked about that with me. I'm sure he set notes down about it; he kept exhaustive records concerning everything about me..." Had Doctor Adlington written about what he and Dmitri had done together? Would Kenneth find the details of it in some dusty notebook? The thought of Kenneth reading those details was... not as embarrassing as it ought to have been. Actually, it made him feel quite warm...

"He kept exhaustive notes but you've never read them?"

"I wasn't supposed to; he said it would spoil the validity of the experiments concerning my development..."

"Strange, that. Not the approach I'd have taken at all, though I'm sure Uncle must have had his reasons. I'll have to go over his notes," Kenneth said absently, peeling out of his overcoat. He turned back to Haider, seeking some reaction. His eyes were keenly intelligent; brown, and warm, and openly assessing him. And it was quite suddenly intolerable. It was madness to mention it, but Kenneth was likely to find out in any case, and then what would he think of Haider's reticence on the subject? Kenneth might put him away again. Might disassemble him to explore the problem. Worse, Kenneth might take it as a challenge and attempt to repair whatever flaw there was in Haider's mind that made him curious about such things. But... but if he was to be put away again it was surely better to have it done with...

"I... There was a reason that I was put away," Haider confessed, his hands shaking slightly.

He found the story wrenching its way out of him word by word, almost against his volition. Once started, he couldn't stop telling Kenneth about Dmitri. About how much he'd enjoyed it. About how he knew objectively that this wasn't the appropriate response and how he didn't give a damn...

And Kenneth listened attentively. The only outward sign he gave at all to Haider's confession was a slight reddening of his cheeks. There was silence for several long minutes before Kenneth replied.

"That's... quite alright then. I certainly..." he ran a hand through his hair, disarranging it horribly, and smiled quickly before looking away. "In any case, no one need know about that unless you'd like them to. If there are notes detailing... the... incidents... they can certainly be edited from any final publications."

And for a week thereafter, there was no more talk of it.

Haider was introduced to Kenneth's colleagues and students at Harvard, and was very well received. There was some discussion of his taking quarters at the university, but nothing ultimately came of it, as he preferred to spend his nights in Kenneth's study. In a week's time he learned more from Kenneth's notes than most undergraduate students of mechanoscience could claim. To be fair, he did have a rather unfair and personal knowledge of such things.

The situation was altogether tolerable, and yet he found himself discontented. It had taken him the better part of a day to place it. There was a sadness about Kenneth that Haider wanted to soothe. He wanted to take Kenneth into his arms and hold him... comfort him. More than that, he wanted to show him pleasure. He wanted to do whatever was necessary to drive that perpetual sadness from his eyes. It was more than he could bear; Kenneth was so damnably casual around him, so close. They touched frequently—a hand laid on his shoulder, a leg pressed against his own on a bench while they studied some small mechanism—and he couldn't help but envision more. He wanted to run his hands along Kenneth's lean, muscled body...What would it feel like for those delicate, capable hands to caress him?

It was something that he was going to have to address quite soon.

———●———

KENNETH WAS UTTERLY miserable. He wondered, absently, if it wouldn't be better to return to Europe and put the distance of an ocean between himself and Haider, leaving the marvel of him to more capable and less deviant mechanoscientists.

He acknowledged now that his desire to lay hands on Haider was more than scientific in nature. It had nothing at all to do with his interest in his mechanisms.

Haider, at present, was attending a talk being given by one of Kenneth's fellows from the university. Kenneth had elected not to attend on grounds of continuing work on his most recent project, but the reality was that he found himself needing to spend more and more time away from Haider. He knew that more than one of his students had observed him gazing at the automaton wistfully. If none had guessed his reasons yet, it was only by luck, or by the general knowledge that Kenneth was more than a little obsessed by the *Ars Mechanica* and touched by the same mad genius as his late uncle...

It was well past dark, and Kenneth was working by the light of an incandescent lantern that cast harsh heat as well as light. His brass goggles prevented the beading sweat of his brow from falling into his eyes, but he feared that his hair must be in a frightful state, considering how frequently he found himself slicking it backward with fingers covered in soot and engine grease. Theoretical mechanoscience was well and good, but it was the sort that left one dirty beneath the fingernails that really satisfied him, that drew him to the craft.

He was thus rather indisposed when Haider found him. He'd discarded his collar and tie, and then his jacket, and now stood in only a partly open white shirt. Haider was still dressed for the university theater, wearing one of Kenneth's borrowed suits, complete with lace cravat and silk top hat. He looked... quite dashing, really. The mask glittered in the incandescent light. He approached with quick steps, looking in brief interest at the parts Kenneth had laid out on the table. When he was close enough that Kenneth could hear the faint whirring and clicking of his internal mechanisms, Haider spoke.

"There's something that we need to address."

That was the only bit of warning Kenneth got before he found himself soundly pressed against the wall, each wrist locked tightly in one of Haider's hands, with Haider looking at him very intently.

"What..."

"Surely you understand that the tension is becoming intolerable, Kenneth," Haider answered simply, a wicked gleam in his eyes. All Kenneth could do was stare dumbfounded as the automaton leaned forward and kissed him...

Kenneth found himself suddenly weak-kneed and very grateful for the length of Haider's body pressing him against the wall. Haider's tongue made its way gently into his mouth, first begging entrance by running along his lip. When Kenneth gasped that tongue plunged into his mouth, flicking across his teeth in bold exploration. Haider tasted of candied violets, and the barest hint of sweet almond. When Haider released his hands they found their way, quite without conscious assistance, to the back of Haider's head. Beneath the soft curls the curve of his skull was warm and very faintly whirring. Kenneth found himself being spun suddenly and forced backward... the backs of his knees contacted the edge of the bench, and he fell heavily. When they finally broke for breath Haider was somehow straddling his lap, the warm weight of him pressing deliciously against Kenneth's flesh with a growing hardness, the fabric of their clothes suddenly a maddening nuisance.

"This is completely unacceptable, you know," Kenneth panted, shifting a bit.

"Whatever you want to tell yourself," Haider countered, his breath intolerably warm against the shell of Kenneth's ear.

"Dear God, don't do that," Kenneth groaned, pushing the automaton away, which proved difficult as Haider wrapped his arms around Kenneth's back and held tight.

"Why not? You want this... and I want you. This only seems the most logical course of action," Haider purred, nosing his way up Kenneth's throat, his breath warm and even. It really was quite a convincing argument.

"It's improper for a gentleman... That is to say..."

"I'm afraid you're over-thinking this situation, Kenneth," Haider replied wickedly, punctuating his words with a sudden tilt of his hips that brought his manhood flush with Kenneth's own.

Kenneth shuddered, letting his head fall back under the following assault of wet, nibbling kisses. Haider flexed his thighs, pressing himself rhythmically against Kenneth. It was so much more than he could stand...

"If you insist on this course of action, I do believe that we're over-dressed," he murmured, running his hands along the automaton's smooth shoulders, down the flat planes of his chest and the tight muscles of his abdomen through the crisp cotton of the borrowed shirt he wore. His fingertips found the hem and then his hands returned upwards, against the supple smoothness of Haider's leather skin. He was met with a purr of satisfaction and Haider obligingly began to unbutton his shirt with a playful slowness. By the time he carelessly let it slip from his shoulders and drop to the floor, Kenneth found his mouth quite dry.

"Now Kenneth, you've already seen me in a far more dire state of undress than this. I do believe it's only fair that you return the favor."

And then he began to unbutton Kenneth's shirt as well. His fingertips were hotter and smoother than a man's should be, and seemed to vibrate with tightly pent energy, humming with the gyros that ran through each of his mechanical joints. He found himself quite helpless as Haider ran those hands possessively across his newly exposed flesh, paying particular attention to dusky pink nipples. He thumbed one, and Kenneth arched, his head thrown back, feeling his face flush.

"I think we should move to a better location. The bedroom comes to mind," Haider teased, sliding one leg carefully sideways and breaking their intimate contact. Kenneth found his head just slightly clearer, and was able to swallow and nod and stagger to his feet at Haider's urging.

"You do realize that this is unnatural," Kenneth murmured, trying to collect himself and turn his thoughts back to reason. He was being pulled by the hand through his own house.

"And why should that matter to me, Kenneth? I'm not a natural creation, now am I?"

"But... sodomy!"

"Is great fun, I assure you."

Kenneth recalled, suddenly, how Haider had gained this knowledge and was thus distracted when he was suddenly pushed to fall back against his bed. Haider was standing above him with his hands on his hips, positioned between Kenneth's knees, regarding him with keen interest. A small smile played at his lips. The light in the bedroom was golden: gaslight that had flickered on automatically with the coming of darkness. In this light Haider looked less an automaton and more a fallen angel or some bacchanalian godling. The utter physical perfection of a classical statue come to life. Gray eyes twinkled behind the ornate mask, challenging.

He descended like a beast upon a kill.

Kenneth found his mind slipping away as the sensations overtook him. Haider's tongue danced across his chest, and he moved lower, trailing downward across quivering muscles. Deft fingers unbuttoned his trousers, and then there was the inexorable connection of flesh with flesh... a gust of hot air across his straining manhood, and his eyes opened wide in shock as he realized what was coming an instant before it happened...

And then Haider's mouth was upon him, and he was undone.

Nothing in his life had ever felt so damnably exquisite... oh, he'd never known. The act wasn't new to him, he'd certainly heard about it in less polite circles. He'd given it much consideration. But of the handful of girls he'd shared intimate relations with, none had ever been so improper as to suggest such a thing. He'd been too much of a gentleman to suggest it himself.

"You wicked machine...." he panted, balling his hands into fists among the satin-smooth bedclothes.

"Haider," he corrected, making hot and cool air dance marvelously over the straining head of his manhood.

"Haider..." Kenneth gasped in agreement, his hips bucking of their own volition as the automaton's tongue ran a quick circle before moving downward to teasingly stroke the underside. His hands were moving again, stroking along Kenneth's inner thighs, drifting butterfly-light across the cusp of each hip, grasping with gentle power and pressing downward when his hips bucked again. He moved just slightly deeper, bringing the head of Kenneth's manhood into contact with something at the back of his throat that fluttered in a way that certainly wasn't humanly possible.

It was too much, and the startling brilliance of release caught him, dragging him up to heady heights of ecstasy and letting him fall. Moments later he opened his eyes to find Haider lying by his side, propped on one arm and watching him intently.

Kenneth's experience with sex had been fairly limited... he'd had certain relations, of course, with a number of young women. With professional women. It had never seemed especially important, but there were times when it had simply seemed impolite to refuse and it wasn't as if the experiences hadn't been pleasant. Still, it had always seemed lacking, somehow. This had been different. This had been the stuff of the torrid dime romances that Kenneth had a rather unhealthy fondness for.

His experience limited as it was, he still knew enough to prove his thanks and at least attempt reciprocation. He turned on his side, edging downward and running his fingers across Haider's chest and belly. Smooth, warm leather taut over brass and steel within. Haider's expression was questioning, and Kenneth grinned at him before taking the head of his manhood into his mouth.

"Ah!" Haider barked, coming up onto his elbows and looking down at Kenneth. Their gazes locked for an instant, and Haider groaned lightly. "You... oh... you don't have to..."

Kenneth pulled back, tilting his head a bit. "Would you like me to stop?"

"If you want to..." Haider started, his reply cut short by a gasp. Kenneth smiled at the permission and continued, pleasure still echoing through him from Haider's attentions. This was deeply satisfying in its own way, hearing Haider's hitched breath, feeling smooth fingertips against his scalp as they slowly worked their way into his hair, holding him to the task...

"I need..." Haider gasped, tugging at his hair. Kenneth looked up to the arresting sight of Haider in desperation, eyes closed behind the mask, lower lip caught between ivory teeth. "I need you. You're so warm, so alive. I need you in me."

Kenneth found himself hauled bodily back up the bed, more or less with his cooperation, and laid firmly on his back. Haider was on his knees, straddling Kenneth's hips with a liquid flexibility that gave him a moment of envy. Haider looked down at him, swallowing thickly between breaths. His eyes were positively glowing, illuminating his face with a pale fire. He was so damned perfect...

And he closed his eyes, throwing his head back in apparent ecstasy as he slowly impaled himself on Kenneth's flesh. He lost all presence of mind then; his world was all cloying heat and delicious friction as Haider rocked his hips. He tossed his head, eyes closed and mouth partly open, a string of small cries bubbling from his throat in counterpoint to the steadily-louder whirring and clicking of his internal mechanisms. He leaned forward, reaching over Kenneth's head to take hold of the headboard, rising up just slightly on his knees and dropping down again. Again. Again. A perfect, mechanical rhythm. He was inhumanly warm, the slick tightness of him impossible, the electric vibration of his internal workings conspiring to drive Kenneth to madness. His cries were addictive, going to Kenneth's head like a strong liquor, making him crave more. Haider shot out a hand with inhuman speed and gripped one of Kenneth's own, drawing it between them to meet the hard and ready length of Haider's manhood. He gripped and began to stroke.

"There...with...with your thumb....ah!" Haider panted, his cry when Kenneth obeyed was loud enough to have the neighbors wondering. He shuddered, a sudden tensing of all his muscles, his cries taking on a new level of desperation. There might have been words in them, they might have been entreaties; they were beyond language now. It was more than Kenneth could stand, and with a shattering brilliance he came. Haider hissed, a sound like an engine releasing a jet of steam, his eyes opened wide and glowing with an intensity that surpassed the gaslights. For a long moment everything was utterly still, silence punctuated by their twinned panting, by Haider's clockwork interior slowing down from its double quickness.

Haider melted down onto Kenneth's chest, his breath warm and even. Kenneth wrapped his arms around his back, holding him there, taking in the faint cedar scent of his hair.

"I want you on top, next time," he said softly. Kenneth shivered, closing his eyes at the thought. At the thought that this would very surely be something they'd have to repeat with a great number of variations. For science.

He really did adore the *Ars Mechanica*.

The Goose Boy

Queen Joan of Conward had two sons. The older son, Conrad, would inherit her kingdom and was brought up as a warrior. He quickly married and just as quickly produced an heir. The younger son, Giles, was brought up to be a learned man, the better to advise his brother one day. When he was twenty, the queen sent him forth to the neighboring kingdom to study under the great master-scholar there, and to keep company in the young king's court.

Giles was as bright as an autumn day, with hair the color of fox fur and eyes like the sky at noon. He was a slight young man; a nimble dancer and a fine rider and much loved by all the court. When he was sent abroad, his mother sent with him a black mare named Falada. The queen had acquired her from a wise woman in her own youthful adventures, and she could speak. Falada was pleasant and patient and wise, but only those of noble birth were able to hear her. The queen also sent a gray mare, and a serving girl named Avelyn to ride her.

Avelyn, unknown to all, was the daughter of a wise and crafty woman and had learned a bit of magic from her mother. No sooner were she and Giles a full day's ride from the castle than she cursed him and took away his powers of speech. When Giles went to bathe, she stole his clothing and gave him rags to wear. In his silence, he could do nothing against her as she told lies in the next city they came to, and she sold all of his fine possessions to buy finery for herself.

"It will be better this way," the girl claimed, combing out her black hair. "What use could a king have for a popinjay like you? I can at least be his bride."

When they arrived at the court of the young king, Avelyn claimed that she was a princess from a foreign land ravaged by war who had been sent to seek asylum in the king's court. She looked very fine in her new attire – plump and well-formed, her skin nut brown and her hair raven black and her eyes the twinkling green of a cat's. She told the stable hand that the black horse had a tendency to kick and bite and that it had given her nothing but trouble and pain – and that it should be immediately butchered. Giles, she said, was nothing but a peasant's foundling upon whom she'd taken pity and kept as a servant. As he was surly and lazy, she had no use for him any longer.

Thus Falada was slain, because the young prince could say nothing in her favor. Yet when he found her bare skull among the pile of offal, he found that being slain bothered her not at all and that she spoke as pleasantly and patiently as she ever had. Nor did she have any trouble understanding him in his silence.

"Well. This has gone very badly indeed, now hasn't it?" Falada said, her voice a whisper in his ear.

'I am bewitched. What else could I have done? If I confronted her, people would only think me mad!' Giles thought back bitterly.

"You're probably right. I wouldn't know. Things have always been that much simpler for me than they are for you humans. Still, I suppose you'll have to make do as best you can and find yourself some employment, lest you starve."

'While she courts the king and sits by the arm of the scholar,' Giles replied in silence.

"You'll gnaw yourself hollow. I dislike this place; take me somewhere dry at least. Death, I think, may be a troublesome thing."

And so Giles found himself a job as a goose-tender. He was paid in daily bread, and given a pallet of straw in a barn. He hung Falada's skull on the wall, and the servants around him reckoned it was a pagan gesture and generally avoided him.

So it went for a fortnight. Giles rose at dawn and chased a flock of geese in and out and all around the town with a stick, reciting Latin in his head to prevent his mind from going numb. In the evenings he conversed at length with Falada on the subjects of philosophy or astronomy or whatever came most readily to mind until he slept.

But then one evening... there was a change.

Giles was slowly nursing his daily cup of ale in the common room where servants ate. A man sat down heavily beside him and started speaking without meeting his eyes.

"Just thought you should know it, lad: he's got his eye on you. Wouldn't do to be... uncivil, if you'll take my advice on the subject. Don't care if you are a wizard or whatever devilshines folks are talking about. You cross him, and you'll wish you hadn't."

And before Giles could think of anything to do to get the man to clarify, he'd stood again and walked off into the crowd. Giles found himself scanning the room for... anyone, really. Not knowing who he was looking for or why anyone should have any interest in him.

There was a man standing in the corner, watching him. Watching him very intently.

He was dressed in the clothes of a merchant, and he wore a long cloak with a hood. Giles could see his eyes flashing from within the shadows of it, warmly brown and uncomfortably direct. When they met his own, the hooded man grinned with a flash of white teeth. Giles looked into his cup studiously.

He approached. Giles held his ground; the warning had been brief and maddeningly cryptic, but he wasn't the sort of man who ran away. The hooded man sat down on the bench beside him, very close. Close enough that Giles could feel the heat of him.

"I'm told that you can't speak," the man said. His voice was smooth and clear; a young man's voice – one that demanded attention. Giles shook his head slightly without looking up.

"Can't, or won't?"

At that Giles did look up, scowling slightly, sighing through his nose. The man who stared back at him was... arresting. The face of an angel gazed at him from the shadows of that hood, framed in dark curls. He'd never seen an angel, painted or otherwise, with so much hunger in its eyes. Giles shuddered, because the intense scrutiny he suddenly faced stirred something low in his belly that was probably best left undisturbed...

"My name is Thom. Walk with me," he said, standing and then offering a hand. His tone was light, but Giles recognized an order when he heard one. Thom had a voice that demanded obedience.

So Giles took his hand and walked with him, out of the common room and down a hallway that he was unfamiliar with. He hadn't had occasion to explore the lower parts of the castle; his work didn't take him there. Thom was sure of his path and clearly had some idea of his destination.

"I haven't seen you here before. You're new, aren't you?" Thom asked casually as they turned a corner. Giles realized that he was quite lost now, and they were well past the sounds of other people... he nodded warily.

"I'm sorry that I don't know your name...but I will confess that I've been watching you for a few days. Forgive my rudeness. It's been most difficult to track you down in the evenings. There are those who say you're a conjurer of some kind. Are they right?"

Giles tried to reply and was reminded harshly that he could not. He rolled his eyes and shook his head.

"You haven't always been without a voice." Not a question. Giles shook his head again.

Thom pushed back his hood. The light here was dim, with moonlight coming in through a single window high on the wall, painting him in smooth planes of black and silver. Dark hair, flashing teeth. Dark eyes with something burning behind them.

"You're very interesting, goose-boy," he breathed, taking a step closer. It was narrow hallway. If Giles stepped back, he would be against the wall. He stood his ground. Thom apparently took that as challenge, because he took another step and suddenly his face was only inches from

Giles' own. His eyes held Giles captive as effectively as any iron chains. The way he looked at him... and truly saw. Not at his body, not at his face, not even at his eyes but into them. Oh, trickery, sorcery, wicked magic... he was looking at Giles and seeing the whole of him, everything that made him. And those eyes, seeing into his own, were hungry. In a final lunge, Thom closed the gap between them and pulled Giles into a burning kiss.

Giles felt his knees give way. That was of no consequence, because Thom deftly caught him and together they shuffled backward until the inexorable strength of cold stone was at Giles' back, a sharp counter-point to Thom's heat. His mouth tasted like wine and burned like fire. When they broke for breath Giles found himself gasping, tilting his head back to grant Thom easy access to his neck. Lips and tongue and teeth descended there, marking a burning path downward to the hollow of his throat. One of Thom's hands was tucked at the small of his back, but the other moved in a broad stroke across Giles' chest and belly and then downward to caress him in a wholly indecent way. His breath left him in what would have been a moan if he'd had a voice.

Thom pulled his other hand free, both of them alighting on Giles hips, and their eyes met again.

"May I?" he breathed.

Giles nodded frantically.

Thom dropped to his knees and proceeded, with the kind of deftness that could only come from long practice, to unlace Giles' breeches and free him to the cool of the night air. He moved without preamble to devour Giles whole.

By all the gods he knew, it had never been so good.

One broad and callused hand gripped the base of his length firmly, the other wandered as it pleased along his stomach, his thighs, between them to stroke and cup and gently squeeze... and all the while that mouth worked its hot, wet, utterly wicked magic. Thom was thorough enough to be deeply satisfying, teasing enough to make it worthwhile, and he commanded every breath and stroke and purring vibration with expert sureness. There wasn't a moment of hesitation or uncertainty in him.

Giles was a prince. No one had ever so thoroughly commanded him before... no one had dared. But he was only a goose boy here. Whoever Thom was, he certainly appreciated that fact and behaved accordingly. Treated him like some base-born plaything...

Thom took Giles to the hilt in one long agonizingly slow bob of his head, and he swallowed, and Giles was done for. His head arced back as he came, cracking against the wall with enough force to have him seeing stars, and were it not for the strength of Thom's hands on his hips he might have crumpled to the floor. As it was he was lost for several long moments, riding the waves of his climax as Thom drank from him and moaned in earnest, pulling back to lay his face against Giles' thigh, his panting breath hot and cold at once as it gusted across slick, sensitive flesh. Giles found himself sinking to his knees under Thom's guidance, then sitting on his heels, then being fiercely kissed again.

"Meet me tomorrow, at sunset, at the gatehouse. I'll make it worth your time," Thom whispered into his ear... and then he was standing, pulling away. Footsteps ringing with quickness in the empty corridor.

And then he was gone, leaving Giles alone in the darkness, his head still swimming.

Giles knew an order when he heard one.

It was less difficult than he'd first imagined to find his way back to the barn where he was currently quartered, his mind still reeling from what had just happened. He felt distinctly used, but... he found that he didn't mind in the slightest. Was this the lot of the base-born then? To be so commanded by the whim of the gentry? He knew from hearsay that such dalliances were not uncommon. He'd simply never seen occasion to try any such thing himself His mother's court had no lack of gentle-born young men who were only too eager to secure an attendance with a prince. Giles climbed the ladder to his loft and fell against his bed in exhaustion, gazing at bare beams of the roof.

"You're very late to bed this night, my prince," Falada's whisper-voice said wryly.

'Yes, I am,' he replied in thought, sparing her a glance. She was grinning, as skulls were wont to do, and she only kept grinning and said nothing more.

Giles was preoccupied in his work the following day, and if the geese didn't make their rounds as thoroughly as usual then at least no one berated him for it. Sunset couldn't come quickly enough.

Giles had forgone his supper to wait by the gatehouse, and he was beginning to wonder if he'd been foolish to do so. The setting sun took the warmth of the day with it. The guards in the tower above, while they hadn't said anything to him directly, had certainly offered him more than one critical glance as he stood there by the gate. He was too far from them to hear their conversation, but he had seen one point him out to the other.

And then someone tapped him on the shoulder and he spun to find Thom standing there with a wolfish smile. No idea how he'd managed to get so close without Giles noticing. It was... unsettling.

Thom produced a key from his pocket and proceeded to open the door at the bottom of the tower. Giles was beginning to wonder just who he was that he had access to such a thing, and if it was achieved in any legitimate fashion, but he lacked the capacity just now to ask questions.

He was led up a set of narrow, curving stairs to a small room midway up the tower. Two men were sitting at a table, playing cards. They looked up sharply when Thom entered, and one of them paled.

"Leave," Thom said with that same perfect authority.

The men glanced at one another, and at Giles, but they did as they were told without hesitation.

The room Giles found himself in was appointed with a table and chairs, a number of candle lamps, two narrow windows, and a bed. Thom locked the door.

"We have more time tonight," Thom said as he turned to face Giles, taking his cloak off and hanging it on the wall. "No one is expecting me back."

Giles stood, his arms crossed, watching. In this light Thom was pale gold, his hair the color of sable. He noted Giles' scrutiny and smiled, standing with his hands on his hips and inviting further inspection.

"Take your clothes off," he ordered coolly.

Giles narrowed his eyes, keeping his arms folded.

"If you won't, I could do it for you," Thom said, his voice challenging. Giles turned his head slightly, looking at Thom sideways, a small smile playing at his lips. Thom was abruptly at his side, moving with a swiftness Giles could hardly warrant. Close enough that they shared breath. Close enough that he was caught in the endless depths of those burning brown eyes again.

Giles offered no resistance as Thom began unlacing his shirt. It was quickly discarded. When Thom tried to unlace his breeches, Giles caught him by the wrists and took a step back, narrowing his eyes. Thom met his gaze, apparently confused, and Giles offered a mischievous smile and pointed at him.

"Ah, so you wish to keep things equitable?" Thom asked with a wry smile. Giles nodded.

"You don't know who I am, do you?"

Giles shook his head.

"All the better," Thom said, offering a predatory smile as he began to unlace his own shirt with agonizing slowness. Giles watched, his mouth going a bit dry. Thom was all smooth skin and solid muscle, a body that spoke of.... prowess. His white merchant's shirt was tossed carelessly into a corner, and he met Giles' eyes with a spark of challenge when it was gone, fingering the laces of his own breeches for a moment before unlacing those as well.

And Giles was never one to allow a favor to go unreturned.

He dropped to his knees and moved upon Thom in eager appreciation, letting the hot, hard length of him slide along his cheek before taking the head into his mouth. Thom nested broad hands into his hair, holding him to the task, purring in satisfaction as Giles laid his hands on his thighs. Thighs that were still cased in smooth leather.

Giles hadn't often pleasured other men with his mouth; he was far more often on the receiving end of such attention... but he wanted very much to please Thom. It wasn't something he could distinctly name, but there was such delicious authority to the man. Such... nobility. He found himself achingly hard and relished the feeling, purring deep in his throat. There was no sound to it, but Thom's moan proved that it was still quite effective.

"You're good at this," Thom observed breathlessly, thighs turned outward, mouth partly open, eyes closed. "Might... have to keep you... closer..."

Giles ran his hand upwards, fingernails grazing lightly at the taut-stretched leather at the juncture of Thom's thighs. Thom bucked, pressing forward, and Giles suddenly found himself nosing dark curls and swallowing frantically as Thom came at the back of his throat.

He panted, swallowing, feeling a dizzy sort of satisfaction as Thom collected himself...and then he was quite suddenly caught under the arms and hauled upward into a fierce embrace. The room spun and Thom turned him and skittered back three paces and suddenly he was on his back on the bed and Thom was on top of him and he was being brutally, wonderfully kissed.

Thom was unlacing his breeches with frantic, fumbling hands without breaking their kiss. Giles found that he had to resort to doing sums in his head to counteract just how deucedly appealing that was. His breeches were soon discarded, leaving them both naked. Thom was on his knees and straddling him, gazing down at him in open appreciation.

And then a hot hand, hard with a swordsman's calluses, closed on his arousal.

Thom ran his thumb in a quick circle around the head, spreading the slickness there, and Giles' breath left him in a stuttering sigh.

"If I make you come, do you think you'll still be able to fuck me later?" Thom asked, a predatory fire in his eyes. The question became moot, because the obscene suggestion of it was more than Giles could bear and he bucked in Thom's fist, the purest of pleasure rolling through him as his seed spilled forth, splashing against his own chest and belly. Thom laughed.

And when he bent to lap the evidence of open lust from Giles' flesh, the answer to his question soon became apparent. By the time Thom reached his sack and took one ball and then the other into his mouth, he was hard and desperately wanting again.

"I need to fetch the oil. Wait," Thom said, rising from him. The loss of his touch was like a blow, and Giles found himself turning to watch as he crossed the room. Thom moved with catlike grace, silver moonlight from the windows and golden light from the candles working in concert to play a beguiling dance of light and shadow across the muscles of his back.

He returned in due course with a vial of oil, which he immediately put to good use. Giles fell against the bed again as Thom's callused hands slicked down the length of him, pausing to palm the head.

"I need you on your knees," he said, his voice thick and his eyes half-lidded. Giles was in no mood for teasing defiance. He obediently rose and Thom slipped into bed just in front of him, facing away. He gripped the foot board in both hands and looked over his shoulder at Giles, his face an open challenge.

Giles was more than happy to meet it.

He positioned himself and pressed inward with one smooth stroke, and Thom's moan of satisfaction rang against the walls. Giles lost himself in the delicious friction, Thom's flesh tightening around him beautifully, and he threw his head back and gasped. He was supposedly some base-born nobody now, and here he was having his pleasure of a noble... who had demanded such in no uncertain terms. He wondered for a moment what this man would think of him if he knew that Giles was a prince...

"Harder," Thom groaned, his shoulders tensing under Giles' hands.

Giles followed the order he was given, doubling his efforts, ducking his head to explore the juncture of Thom's neck and shoulder with lips and teeth and tongue. He snaked a hand downward, finding Thom's hard length and gripping it, pumping it in time with his thrusts. Thom gave an incoherent cry, bucking hard enough to lift them both off the bed, coming down again hard and taking Giles to the hilt. He tilted his head away to give Giles greater access, and Giles continued tonguing and nipping, his breath coming in sharp gasps.

"Want this... every night!" Thom said, his voice a bark, a growl. And he came, the wet heat of him splashing over Giles' fist like pleasant fire, his flesh tightening almost painfully, and Giles shuddered and spilled himself deep inside him.

There was a quiet dissolution after that as they untangled themselves, falling into a jumble of sweat-slick limbs on the bed, both spent to utter exhaustion. Thom was purring into his ear between panting breaths, a sound of pure satisfaction. Giles turned fractionally to kiss him, and their kiss was long and slow and sweet.

"I'll come for you again tomorrow," Thom whispered, pulling him close. Giles smiled, and would have murmured agreement at the suggestion if he'd had the voice to do so.

They slept.

It was dark when Giles woke to movement. By moonlight he watched Thom sitting at the edge of the bed, donning his clothes.

"I can't stay, though I wish I could," he said, looking at Giles with an odd pain in his eyes. "Would that I could bring you with me... but I'll come for you again tonight. Here. You can go back to sleep if you want; no one will bother you here and it's still hours until dawn."

Giles nodded slowly, settling back against the bed. Thom leaned over him and kissed him as deeply and thoroughly as anyone ever had. There was such hunger in that kiss, such desperate longing. It was a kiss that asked, begged, pleaded... and Giles knew in that moment that he would give anything Thom asked of him, and do so willingly.

And for the second time in as many nights, Thom left him in the darkness.

He woke again to the songs of morning birds and the sounds of the city waking. In a guard tower, like a common whore... but there had been so much passion these last nights. More than he'd ever known when he lived in a palace. He'd have to think long on this... here he sat, deserted by the world. A queen's son, forced to fulfill the office of goose-boy, while a waiting-maid sat on the king's right hand. If his mother only knew...

But damn him for a fool if it didn't seem worth it for what the nights brought now.

He gathered his scattered clothing, slightly dismayed at the state of it, but he had nothing better to wear. Well, he doubted the geese would give a damn.

He was walking down the narrow lane that led from the tower to the servants' hall when a man in guards' livery barred his way with a mischievous smile.

"And what's a pretty bit like you doing walking this way at this hour, hmm?"

Giles flushed, knowing how he must appear. He ducked and tried to step aside, but the guard matched him.

"Now, now. It's early yet. Won't anyone mind if I'm a few minutes late for my watch..."

"Hugh, leave him," a voice said behind him, making Giles spin. Another guard, one of those who'd been in the room before Thom had dismissed them. Giles felt himself flush even further.

"And why should I?" The first guard said, indignant. "I know well enough where he's come from and there's no reason you night watch should have all the fun..."

"He's King Thomas' new favorite."

Giles suddenly felt rather dizzy. The guard stood aside, and he staggered past. King Thomas. Thom. He'd been dallying with royalty and he hadn't even known.

He walked in a haze to the common room and broke his fast on bread and milk. Damn the geese. He returned to his barn and climbed the ladder, a thousand thoughts clattering in his head like squabbling ravens.

"You didn't return to bed at all last night, my prince," Falada's voice said coolly. He turned to look at her hanging there on the wall, her empty eyes seeming to regard him.

'He's the king.' Giles thought back, unable to collect himself more eloquently.

"Whom?"

'Thom. Thom's the king. I've been...'

"Well then, I suppose that your troubles will soon be solved. You have audience with the person best able to set rights the situation you find yourself in. You need only get him to speak to me and I can explain your troubles."

Ah, but what would Thom... or rather, King Thomas, think upon knowing the truth? He thought he was dallying with a goose-boy so lowly that he didn't even require a name. When he learned that Giles was a prince of Conward...

Still, there was little choice left before him. The situation had to be set to rights.

Giles had half a mind to simply bring Falada with him when he went to the gatehouse, but he thought better on it when he considered the way that the townsfolk crossed themselves at his passing as it was. That he hung a horse's skull on the wall was common knowledge and tolerated, but carrying one about with him as he skulked through the streets at night would probably be met with unpleasant ramifications.

So he waited at the gatehouse again as he had the previous night, arms crossed and much on his mind. The sun set. Darkness fell. Giles sat against the wall, chewing on his thumbnail.

It was an hour before Thom arrived, looking weary and worn. Giles rose to his feet at the sight of him, hedging his eyebrows.

"I don't know if I'm even able..." Thom began, but Giles hushed him with narrow fingers placed against his lips, and Thom's weary eyes lit with curiosity.

Giles took his hand and pointed toward the alley that led to the servants' hall.

"We can't go there."

Giles shook his head impatiently, tugging on Thom's hand.

"I tell you, we cannot. I cannot," Thom insisted, his eyes flashing anger. Giles set his jaw, sighing through his nose, and turned on his heel and walked away.

"Come back here!" Thom called indignantly. Giles stopped, looking back over his shoulder, and tossed his head in the suggested direction.

"I could call the guards down on you," Thom warned.

It was Giles' turn to stare challenge at him, and as he watched Thom narrowed his eyes and bared his teeth, and followed Giles into the darkness. Past the servants' hall, to the barn. Up the ladder.

He startled when he saw Falada's skull, and if Giles hadn't caught his hand he might have fallen from the ladder when she spoke.

"Greetings, King Thomas. Our meeting is long overdue," she said with the sound of a smile in her voice. Giles sat with his legs drawn up and his arms around his knees as Thom listened to Falada recounting the story of their misfortune. Of Avelyn's treachery.

"That unforgivable wench has been making my court a hell since she arrived. Nothing pleases her. She...she wants to marry me! And she's so viciously sweet with her words that the court listens to her pleas... I have no heirs, and never mind that my younger brother in Northmere already has four sons! You have no idea how glad I am..." Thom paused, looking at Giles, and swallowed thickly. "Both of you must come at once to the palace. I'll have my royal conjurer awakened."

And so with Falada tucked under his arm, Giles was led to the palace in Thom's company. The conjurer was awakened; a woman of later middle years who took one look at him, sighed through her nose, and said simply,

"Speak, child!" as she made a small gesture. She looked at the skull and said, "I'm sorry, Milady, that there's nothing I can do for you."

And then she turned around and closed her door.

"I ought to be rid of that woman," Thom spat, preparing to knock on the door again.

"I don't know..." Giles said, his voice hoarse from disuse. "She seems to know what she's doing."

"Yes, but -" Thom began, then caught himself and spun to meet Giles' eyes with surprise and joy. "Your voice."

"I'm no longer bewitched," Giles said, so unused to speaking that it felt strange to do so.

"The state of you, though. You must come at once and bathe, and dress as befits your station."

"I would appreciate it if I could be left out of that," Falada said mildly, a hint of knowing smugness to her whispery voice.

Falada was left on the mantle in the king's own chamber, and it was to the king's private baths that Giles was led.

"I had no idea that you were a prince," Thom said in a voice barely above a whisper as the door closed behind them.

"And I had no idea that you were a king," Giles replied, turning to face him boldly. "Does that... change things?"

"Well," Thom said carefully, "It would only befit your station to sit at my side and dine at my table and be quartered close to me."

He met Giles' eyes, and there was a familiar hunger there.

"I do believe that I'd find that very agreeable," Giles replied, and punctuated his words by slipping out of his clothes. Thom followed suit and led him to a marble basin that was easily large enough for both of them.

He'd quite forgotten how good hot water could feel. And soap...especially when that soap was applied by the capable hands of a startlingly attractive young man who also happened to be the king.

Thom pulled him into a fierce embrace, hot and wet and achingly powerful. His hands were everywhere, as if they meant to map every inch of Giles' skin.

"You really don't know what it means to me that... that this is real. That you're real. That you're noble. That I..." Thom faltered, not meeting his eyes.

"That you can have me," Giles finished for him, a smile tugging at his lips as he nested his hands in Thom's hair and guided him into a long, slow kiss. Thom moaned into his mouth, a desperate noise. Giles pulled away long enough to turn around, Thom embracing him from behind, drawing a soap-slick hand across his chest to graze his hardened nipples. Giles leaned against the edge of the basin, his feet planted wide.

"You want..."

"Yes."

Thom moaned again softly, kissing Giles just below the point of his jaw. Giles purred appreciation, heat pooling low in his belly. He felt Thom's length, hot and hard, pressing into him. Thom's hands grasped his hips powerfully... it was a slow, impossible melding of flesh as he was stretched and filled. His fingers splayed out on the cool marble, anchoring him to reality as Thom began to move. His thrusts were slow, delicious, maddening and perfect. The tile under Giles' hands was cool, the water around them hot, Thom's length within him even hotter. Giles arched against him, and he shifted slightly, and suddenly every stroke brushed past that spot within him that made him see stars.

Giles had forgotten how loud his voice could be.

Thom was shushing him, the bursts of warm breath hot against the shell of his ear, and he gasped. A broad hand came down along his chest and belly to find and take hold of him in a firm grasp. The water moved across his length in counterpoint to Thom's thrusts, to his pumping fist, and Giles surrendered himself to the sensations. He laid his forehead against the cool marble, and he bit his lip, and he came with a shattering brilliance. He didn't know how much longer it was when he came back to himself, but Thom was facing him, kissing him, holding him close in the swiftly-cooling water.

"Sleep in my bed," Thom ordered with all the authority of a king.

"Yes, your majesty," Giles answered with a smile. "For as long as you'll have me."

Daylight came, and Giles was dressed in royal apparel. Thom remarked upon the improvement it made in his appearance, and his eyes made promises about just what he'd have liked to do if more pressing matters hadn't been at hand.

A great banquet was prepared, and the young king sat at the head of the table with the lovely but shrewish foreign princess at his side. Giles stood at the doorway, waiting for his cue.

Just before the banquet began, when everyone was merry with anticipation, Thomas turned to Avelyn and asked,

"Milady, suppose that there was a criminal who had deceived everyone in his midst..." and proceeded to a thinly-veiled version of Giles' misfortune. Avelyn smiled blithely through it, nodding occasionally, eyes upon the roast goose. Her inattention was plain, as was Thom's annoyance. Thom finished with, "What sentence should be passed?"

"Such a wretch deserves no better fate than to be stripped entirely naked, and put in a barrel which is studded inside with pointed nails. Two white horses should be harnessed to it and should drag it along through one street after another until the damned criminal is dead," Avelyn answered with a light sweetness that belied the poison of her words. The room fell to silence as King Thomas stared at Avelyn like a landed fish for an entire minute.

"I would not envy the realm that has you for its queen, you horrible, vicious little chit," he finally said. "But then, no realm will have to tolerate such a tragedy." Thom grinned and snapped his fingers, and the footman stepped forward and said clearly,

"Presenting Giles Prince of Conward, second son of Queen Joan."

The color drained from Avelyn's face as Giles stepped forward and bowed slightly.

"Prince Giles, I'll ask the same question of you. To what punishment should such a faithless wretch be put?"

"I do believe that such a person should be cursed with the removal of their voice for a year and a day, so as to learn humility," Giles answered, locking his gaze of Avelyn's. "And I think that they should be sent back to the land of their origin and presented to the keepers of law there."

"That strikes me as most noble and just, Prince Giles," Thom said with a small smile. "Guards? If you would remove this woman to the custody of my conjurer?"

And so Avelyn was removed of her voice and sent back to Conward, with a retinue of guards to make sure that she caused no further mischief on the journey, and a letter of explanation for the queen.

Giles sat at the king's side and studied with the master scholar, as his mother had intended, though if his mother only knew...

In any case, when Avelyn's sentence was carried out, Giles sat at the king's right hand as his best and most trusted advisor, and together they reigned over the kingdom in peace and happiness for the rest of their days.

A Goblin in Hand

I watched the mage shoot my master. I felt his blood as it landed on my face.

That sidhe had been my master. Now he was dead. He deserved to be—I didn't feel bad about that. But now there was a human facing me. He'd killed my master...so now he was my master. He leveled the gun at me. It could end now, if I wanted it that way.

But I wanted to live, so I looked up and him and said,

"Please...I'll do as you say..."

I was on my feet again, at least. I'd dropped when I heard gunfire, and my legs didn't want to listen. Walking wasn't going to happen, I realized with sudden dismay. If I tried to pick my foot up I was going to fall. Wasn't even that I wanted to be defiant. Gods no, I wanted so much to obey. To prove that I deserved to live.

"What's your story?" the mage demanded. He kept the gun pointed at me with the one hand, but used the other to push back his hood. He had dark hair, pulled back harshly from his face. I tilted my head back to get a good look at him, and knew at once that had been a mistake; he caught me with his eyes—nasty, thoroughly human trick. His eyes were piercing, like a serpent's, and they pinned me down to stillness. They could see right through me. Right into me.

"I'm yours now," I answered without even thinking about it.

"What?"

"I'm blood-bound. He was my master; you killed him, now I'm bound to you. You can either kill me or let me serve you. I'll do as you say...Master."

"Face down, hands on your head."

It had all the strength of an order, and I was powerless to disobey. I would have done so anyway, because it was plain relief to be off my feet. We'd been running for days, my master and I. Well, my former master. I heard the mage moving...he was searching the sidhe's corpse. I heard him chanting and saw the flash and the smelled brimstone as he destroyed the body with alchemical fire.

"You know if the information in his wallet's any good? The address on his ID, he actually live there?"

"I don't know, Master. The haven is on Pasthook Street. I can show you."

"Even I'm not crazy enough to go poking my nose into an sidhe's haven after dark. You're coming with me for tonight. We can work out what I'm gonna do with you tomorrow."

"Yes, Master."

"And don't call me that. I don't keep slaves."

"I am bound to you," I said between my teeth. I was still face down on the rooftop, with my hands still on my head, because he hadn't yet told me that I could move. "The only way to be rid of me is to kill me. Master."

He stuck his toe under me and flipped me over in a single sharp movement, standing over me. He had to be better than six feet tall, big even for a man. I felt my ears go back as he stared down at me. Death would be better than having a mage for a master, surely. What mages could do was far, far worse than simple death. Mages could strip the soul. Cleansing, they called it. Rob the mind of wits and sense and self and leave a smiling shell that was blindly loyal and thoughtlessly obedient. I'd seen the cleansed before.

He pulled a length of twine out of his pocket. It was plied red and gray...and given that he was a mage and plainly a fae-hunter, I didn't doubt for a minute that it was rowan twine.

"Get up."

I did. He tied my hands behind my back then walked a circle around me, openly assessing. I stood still for it, but I couldn't keep my tail from lashing like an angry cat's. Damned thing had a mind of its own.

"What's your name?" he asked as he came around in front of me again. I kept my eyes down this time, knowing better than to get caught in his gaze.

"He called me 'Hand'..." I offered hesitantly. A name, a true name, was the most singularly powerful piece of myself that he could take from me. I didn't know much about how one came to be cleansed, but I knew that my name had to be a part of it.

"I didn't ask what he called you, goblin. I asked you your name."

He put his hand out and crooked a finger under my chin, forcing me to look up. To meet his eyes. I didn't want to. Those eyes were entirely too much for me.

His eyes were green, I realized lamely.

"My name is Tarn," I said, breathless, held by his eyes. He smiled, just a little. Satisfaction.

"Tarn," he said. "Sleep."

I went out like a snuffed candle.

I HADN'T KNOWN THE sidhe had a slave. Don't know if it would have changed my plans—the bastard had been a trafficker. A changeling-maker. Someone who stole kids and sold them at the goblin market. The world was a better place without him in it.

But now I had a goblin on my hands...and if he was to be believed, I was damned well stuck with him. It wasn't far-fetched. Free goblins were scarce on the ground since the last Seelie war, and that was ten centuries gone. Most of the survivors were bound into service in one way or another. Most of those were soul-blasted, squeaky clean, into nice, tame house-hobs.

His stature and slimness could have made him childlike, but there was nothing remotely childlike about the goblin who was out cold in the passenger seat of my car. Not quite four feet tall; the top of his head had come to the ` middle of my chest when he'd been standing. He was thin, sinuous. Underfed. His tail, bare except for a trailing tuft of long hair at its tip, was curled along his thigh and laid across his knees. It was quite fascinatingly mobile, even as he slept, and I found my gaze flickering to the side now and again at the movement caught in my peripheral vision. He had long, pointed ears. Those moved too, flicking in response to especially loud radio blips. Parted lips revealed the points of fangs. His skin was cinnamon-colored, marked with darker brown dapples across his cheeks and shoulders. He didn't have a shirt on. Or shoes, for that matter. He was wearing a pair of kid-sized jeans that didn't fit him right. There was probably a story to that.

Deadly little demon-thing. Spawn of dark magics from an older age. Bruised and bloodied and full of such fierce, desperate anger. I saw it there, under all the resignation, and bitterness.

I could certainly find a use for him.

The intelligent thing to do would be to empty his mind before I let him open his eyes. To have him wake and know that I was his master, to have him thoughtlessly obedient. It wouldn't even be hard. I'd never done anything of the kind, but Nathalie had—and she was never one to ignore a phone call from me, no matter what hour it was. It would be the smart thing, because a goblin was dangerous even under the best circumstances. Solid watchdogs, house-hobs could be. Nat had a couple in her lair. I didn't know if Nat's were blood-bound, but I did know she'd wiped them clean right at their capture.

The mindless were damned creepy.

Things in the gloaming didn't work like things in the real world, and you couldn't pass judgment on the former by how things worked in the latter... but slavery didn't sit right with me at all no matter what magic it was wrapped in. Cleansing and misremembering and sight-glamour and all that was even creepier. It wasn't the kind of thing I'd wish on anyone, much less someone who'd already had the crap luck to be bound to an sidhe bastard who snatched babies for a living.

His name was Tarn. He'd told me that just by being asked twice, and I didn't doubt for a minute that it was his true name. Not with how he'd looked at me when he said it. Blood magic was a real and powerful thing, and while there were reasons for him to lie about it, I knew he wasn't. I'd seen it in his eyes as he'd promised to obey me. He had to know what generally became of goblins that fell into the hands of mages. What the consequences of disobedience would be for him. He might well be tractable with nothing more than common courtesy.

And it wouldn't be a chore having someone underfoot who looked this good.

My interest in fae was perverted. I knew that already. I had a thing for short guys. Especially short not-precisely-human guys. The first guy I'd ever hooked up with had been a sidhe.

He was still out cold when I got home. I wasn't going to wake him up until I was ready to deal with him; it was as good a test as any if he really was blood-bound and if he really had given me his true name. I'd ordered him to sleep under the power of both. All things considered, he probably wouldn't wake up until I ordered him to. He looked like he needed the sleep anyhow.

When I picked him up, he made a distressed little noise at the back of his throat; but when I shifted his weight against my shoulder, he tucked his face in at the hollow of my throat and cuddled up against me like it was the most natural thing in the world. He wasn't even awake, and he was touch-hungry. His eyes fluttered open when I wiped the blood off his face, but he wasn't awake. He whined at the back of his throat, and his face followed my hand. I couldn't stop myself. I caressed his cheek with the back of my hand, and he leaned into it with a quiet murmur of appreciation. He offered me his throat, and I caressed him there, too.

I wasn't one to take stupid risks, no matter how helpless Tarn looked. I bound him to the cast-iron frame of my sofa with rowan wood twine—better than cold iron against unseelie fae. That done, well, there was no reason he shouldn't be as comfortable as I could make him. I got him a pillow and a blanket and tried not to be horribly awkward about tucking him in. I'd done too damned much today and there was a lot for me to tie up tomorrow on several different channels. Tarn threw a wrench in all my plans.

But seeing him lying there on my couch, looking exhausted and miserable, I couldn't really blame him for that. I'd just have to figure this out as I went along.

———◆———

I WOKE UP WITH A SENSE of dizzy euphoria, out of what felt like the best sleep of my life. Mild panic followed as I tried to piece together my surroundings, to remember who this human looming over me was.

He'd killed my master. He was my master. I didn't have a name for him yet.

"Well, now we know that works," he said with a smile.

I tried to pull my hands down, found that they were tied above my head, and took a long breath to stifle the panic. All things considered, I was a lot better off than I might have been. I was in full possession of my wits, or at least I felt that way. I was in one piece. Better than I could have hoped for, really, given the circumstances.

"Before I untie you, I've got some questions. You up for answering?"

"Yes, Master."

"I told you not to call me that. My name's Elias. Did some cleaning up and tying down before I bothered to wake you. You've been out for sixteen hours or so; it's Tuesday afternoon. So, concerning this whole blood-bound thing—do you have to do everything I say?"

I didn't know if it was a test or not, but he was looking at me... like I was interesting. Not sizing me up so much as, well, just genuinely curious. Like no one ever was, because I was just a goblin and what was there to wonder about me? Afternoon light was spilling in brilliant and golden and warm, and he was smiling...and he was beautiful. Beautiful in a wholly human way, vital and solid as earth. Inarguably powerful in a way that still managed grace; like a draft horse. Solid, implacable, and casually aware of that. It put me off guard.

"Only if you make it an order, sir," I answered slowly.

"So, say I untied you and just asked you to go get me a beer from the fridge..."

"I could tell you to go get it yourself."

He grinned in response to my theoretical insolence, and his smile broke something inside me. My former master had seldom smiled, and never with such genuine mirth. With such warmth. It set me wanting things I had no business wanting.

He untied me.

"Stay there," he said. Not an order exactly... not even a request. Just an expectation that he'd be obeyed. A test, maybe. I was still contemplating the consequences of refusal when he returned, two bottles dangling from one hand, bottle opener in another. He set one down on the table and sat beside me. The couch shifted under his bulk. He opened one bottle...and he handed it to me.

"This is the part where we spend a long time comparing notes," he said, reaching for the second bottle. "Drink up. I'll hazard a guess and say you deserve it." He opened the second bottle and didn't wait for me to drink before taking a long swallow of his own.

I was speechless for a moment, looking at the bottle in my hand. Nobody gave goblins anything. I looked back at Elias, and he was leaning back on the sofa with his eyes closed.

"I was a changeling, when I was a kid," he said when I failed to say anything. "One of the stolen, I mean. Don't know a thing about my real parents. Brought up as goddamned pet for the vitae juvenales 'til I was about twelve—I started waning down on the vitae. They'd have got rid of me pretty soon, I think. They were just, like, chain-smoking kids—needed to make sure they had a new source before I tapped out completely. They bought another baby on the goblin market, got caught at it, got taken down by a team of mages under Queen Mab. I was way too old to just shuffle back into the mundane world, so the team captain took me home and trained me as her apprentice. Now I work as one of Mab's agents taking out bastards like that guy you were with. Really hope you didn't like the guy or anything."

I snorted, finally taking a sip of the beer he'd given me.

"He was an asshole, deserved what he got," I said. There was a long silence, not especially uncomfortable, while we each drank our beer. "I fought in the last Seelie war. Nobody special, just a pikehead like anyone else. I was captured and got blood-bound. The sidhe are not merciful, and they don't forget—but then, you'd know that. Until the day I die, I belong to someone."

"Sorry there's nothing I can do about that."

"I take it as it comes," I said, leaning back against the sofa. I took another sip. "Not like I haven't had time to get used to it. Some situations are better than others."

He hummed in agreement, but didn't say anything. He just sat back with his arm up along the back of the sofa above my head, eyes closed. Thinking. Or not thinking. He didn't seem like the kind of guy who over-analyzed things. Not a dumb chunk of muscle, certainly, but...relaxed. Easy. The kind of guy who was sure he could handle whatever life threw at him. That was deeply, powerfully comforting.

And what the hell, I might as well see where we stood without all the awkward conversation. I put my empty bottle down and sidled right up next to him. Just to see if he'd let me. I took in his scent—soap and new sweat and wood smoke and the ozone scent of magic. Heard the even, unfaltering rhythm of his heart under my ear. Felt the warmth of his skin.

"Well, aren't you forward," he said, sounding a little surprised. But his hand came down off the back of the couch and slid right onto my shoulder and down the length of my arm and ended up planted on my thigh.

"Testing the waters," I said, leaning into him. He was big. Solid, strong. So much bigger than me, and there was something absolutely perfect about that. Humans were such solid sorts of people. Even sidhe were on the whole bigger than goblins, but humans were another kind of thing entirely—cold iron running in their veins and the crackling vibrancy of vitae thrumming in every fiber of their being. Sidhe could be blind to human vitae once the humans in question were past childhood; goblins most certainly weren't. It was just...humans, and especially mages, were a dangerous lot...and all the more intoxicating for that danger. It was only natural that fae be fascinated. Enthralled and beholden and bewitched. I was painfully aware of all of that as I sat there curled against the man who was my master now.

"You're just taking advantage of the fact that humans are so easily enamored of fae, aren't you?" he teased. But that teasing came with an arm that slipped behind my back and pulled me closer, wrapped right around me and rearranged me so that I was on my knees, straddling his lap.

"Some humans more than others, in my experience, sir," I replied now that his face was inches from mine. He caught me with those eyes again, stopped me short so fast that I had a hard time taking a breath because damn, those eyes were riveting.

"This doesn't have anything to do with being blood-bound, right? Because if..."

"This has to do with you being hot, and me not getting laid in like fifty years," I interrupted. "I'm really hoping you're into goblins. And guys. My guess on both counts is yes, you are."

The hand that was resting at the small of my back slid upward suddenly, up to the back of my neck to pull me forward into a hot, desperate kiss. It had been too damned long. I melted into that kiss as his arms folded around me, pulling me closer, pulling me into the strength and bulk and power of him until my chest was flush with his chest. One hand swept down to cup my ass, fingertips splayed out along the knot of muscle at the base of my tail and that felt better than I'd remembered anything could. Little shocks of pleasant tension ran up my spine with every movement of his fingers, and I broke our kiss by letting my head fall back, giving him my throat. He kept at it, kissing my throat, along the edge of my jaw and up to the point of my ear and dear Gods this man knew what he was doing. He sucked the tip of my ear right inside his mouth and ran his tongue over it. I moaned at that, letting go of the tenuous control I had over this situation. I'd started this, but Elias...my master...most certainly had the upper hand now.

———————◦●◦———————

I HAD HONESTLY NOT expected Tarn to live up to my perverted fantasies, at least not without long and awkward assessment period. I was damned pleased to be wrong in my assumptions as I licked my way along the shell of his ear and took the point into my mouth. He moaned aloud, hot breath gusting against my neck. His hips snapped forward, the bulge in his jeans grinding against my own. I ran my fingers along the underside of his tail until they butted up against coarse fabric, and Tarn made a low sound of abject frustration.

"I hate these pants," he growled into my ear.

"Then take them off," I replied, dragging my nails along the fabric that cased his thighs.

He leaned back, bracing himself against my shoulders and locking his eyes with mine for a long moment, grinning wickedly as his hands went to his fly. His eyes were gold, pupils slitted like a cat's but dilated now into oblong black pools. I was the first to look away, looking down to what he was doing with his hands just in time to have him rise up on his knees and push his jeans downward. He wasn't wearing underwear. He spent longer than was strictly necessary extricating his tail from the hole that had been cut into the seat of his pants for it, running his own fingers along the supple length and very plainly taking pleasure in that. His pants were around his knees, and he wasn't going to get them down any farther without a change of positions. So I turned him around. It wasn't at all fair how easy it was for me to just move him how I wanted, what with him being so little, but he wasn't complaining. I pulled him into my lap and licked my way along the shell of his ear again as he kicked free of his pants. I took advantage of his nudity, running my hands up the insides of his splayed thighs. His tail moved like a serpent, twisting its way down between my legs to mimic what my hands were doing. He leaned his head back against my chest, and I found that he was just the right height to tuck in under my chin; for me to nuzzle into the tousled hair at the crown of his head. I let my right hand close the gap and palmed his balls gently. He gave a long, stuttering moan as I took him in hand, raising his hands over his head to meet at the back of my neck, pulling me down into a position that was only a little awkward for each of us so that I could kiss him again. His teeth were sharp and delicate against my tongue, making me kiss slowly, carefully. He lost his composure entirely, giving way to gasps and moans, when I started stroking him. My own jeans were getting to be a pretty serious problem, but so help me I was going to finish him off before I dealt with it. He was writhing now, moaning and breathless and so impossibly, inhumanely beautiful. Humming with pent energy, power building in his body that could only have one outcome.

"So," I whispered into his ear, "If you have to obey my commands, what happens if I order you to come?"

He moaned long and low, bucking in my hand as he came. He collapsed back against me, panting, purring in his throat with the kind of sound that couldn't come out of anything but a goblin. I wiped my

hand on my pants. I wasn't going to be wearing them much longer anyhow.

⎯⎯➤◉⎯⎯

I HONESTLY COULDN'T remember the last time I'd come that
hard. He'd picked me up, my legs wrapped around his waist and one of
his arms under my ass as he devoured my mouth and moved us...some-
where. I didn't really give a damn where we were going. The destination
became apparent when he laid me down on a bed and stood back to
start stripping with frantic efficiency. I watched the muscles of his abdomen and chest as they came into view, lean and tight. He was scarred
in a couple of places, and I recognized the aftermath of alchemical fire.
He'd seen battle, with sidhe or mages or both, and he'd come through
it alive. A blooded warrior. Pants followed shirt, unzipped gingerly to
free a cock that was almost as big as my forearm.

That most decidedly got my attention, having a human looking
down at me with unabashed lust. Having that human be my master. To
know that he could damned well have anything he wanted out of me.
Bigger than me, more powerful than me, in blood-bound command of
me...and he'd chosen to make this very, very good. To show me pleasure.

He fell back on the bed and pulled me on top of him, drawing me
into another long and desperate kiss. There was so much hunger in his
kisses, and I answered it with hunger of my own. I hadn't realized how
starved for affection I'd been until he'd offered it, and now the need for
touch was running away with both of us. His hands were all over me,
huge and hot and firm and perfect. I halted, helpless, when he started petting and stroking my tail. The end of it curled and lashed of its
own volition, tufted tip brushing my own ankles, brushing his knees. I
moaned against his neck and tried to remember how long it had been
since anyone had touched me like this. He hadn't asked me to do anything yet, and I didn't know if he even wanted me to, but I wanted to
touch him. Wanted to taste him. Wanted to see him come.

I slid down to lay between his thighs and ran both my hands over the length of him. Humans were huge. That was to be expected. Maybe it was that I hadn't been among humans in a really long time, but Elias seemed bigger than he had any right to be. I didn't mind that at all. He stopped dead still when I laid hands on him, his hands on the small of my back and his eyes closed. No suggestion, no request...letting me do whatever I wanted. That was a kind of power that nobody had ever offered me and it left me breathless.

He practically screamed when I put my mouth on him, and stuck his hand in his mouth to quiet himself. I wondered absently if he had neighbors who'd be able to hear.

I could only get the head in my mouth, and I tried to make up for that with my hands. He didn't seem to mind, sitting up enough that he could curl over me and run his hands up and down my back. Run his broad fingertips right down my spine and along my tail... he curled his fingers around the base of it, and suddenly it was joined by the other hand. A hot, wet fingertip pressed against my hole.

"Yes?" he panted.

"Yes," I answered before running my tongue in a circle around the head of his cock.

He pressed forward with that finger in one long, slow stroke. When he was as far as the second knuckle he curled his finger just enough to make lightning shoot up my spine. The hand that was holding my tail eased back, ghosted along my hip, and slipped underneath to find my cock and grip it. I swallowed hard around the flesh in my mouth, and somewhere above me I heard Elias moaning sharply.

He came with a burst of liquid power that was more than I could contend with.

I swallowed and shuddered and hung there between his hands as he toyed with me, his fist pumping in counterpoint to the finger inside me that stroked that spot again and again and again. He shifted a little and then he licked my ear again, along the narrow ridge of it to the point, taking the tip in his mouth and sucking hard and that was that. I came as hard as I had the first time, pressing my face against his thigh and gasping appreciation. There was stillness for a few moment before he pulled his hands back, before he caught me around the waist and laid back and pulled me back on top of him.

We laid like that, with the booming rhythm of his heart pounding under my ear, both of us panting and sweat-slick. He was running his hand lazily up and down my back and it felt so deeply right that I found myself purring.

"Want to join me in the shower?" Elias asked, the vibration of his voice going right to my bones. I grinned stupidly, nuzzling against his chest. I'd have happily stayed right where we were for hours. It was such a long time since I'd been touched and held, and in the glowing aftermath of pleasure the vital humanity of him was like an aura that I was lucky enough to be caught in. Gods, this was why humans were such damnably dangerous things. I was already lost.

"I want to join you wherever you're going," I replied languidly. I got rewarded for the right answer with a kiss. It was a couple more minutes before he finally rolled me off him and got up, stretching his arms over his head. The muscles of his back and ass and thighs when he did that were...perfect.

I got up and followed him where he was leading.

———◆———

HE WAS MINE. THAT WAS only just now sinking in as I watched him soap up his hair. It was really distracting to see how much he enjoyed the shower. I'd had this whole plan that we were going to get clean and dressed and have the whole evening before us to work out...how we were going to work this out.

He was mine. Mine to keep. Mine to do what I wanted with. I was a bad, bad man for finding that appealing. I'd spent too much of my youth among fae to have any kind of proper moral compass...and he was fae. He seemed disconcertingly ok with the whole 'being owned' thing.

I distracted myself with the particulars of getting clean, but having done that it became readily apparent that Tarn had no intention of getting out of the shower until he was told to. He was just standing there under the hot water with this look of pure, simple bliss on his face. Like he wasn't used to showers, in general.

"You're gonna run my water bill through the roof, aren't you?" I said, taking a step forward to stand flush to his back, wrapping an arm around him. He had really nice skin. He leaned his head back against me and hummed in contentment as I ran my hand up and down his chest and belly.

"Hot water's not hooked up back at the haven," he said as I turned the water off and reached for the towels I'd set aside. "My master didn't see the point of it. Comfort breeds weakness and all that."

"Not that 'old code' bullshit," I groaned. "He a twitchy Luddite, too?"

Tarn laughed, and I felt it as much as heard it.

"The works of man are gonna wreck the world, and there's a huge conspiracy behind Mab's rise to power and Morrigan was a better queen and if the chips had just fallen differently during the first Seelie War humans would still be living in caves and cowering under the might of the fae—as they damned well should be, Morrigan's Truth," he said with a deep mock-seriousness.

We dried off and went back to the bedroom. He wrapped the towel around his waist and laid back on my bed, arms folded behind his head, a grin plastered on his face.

"I take it you're not in agreement?" I said, digging through my drawers and pulling out a t-shirt and throwing it at him. I threw on a pair of boxer shorts. When I turned around he'd put the shirt on, and it fell halfway to his knees, which is about what I'd expected. "Gonna have to get you some better clothes."

"Or you could just keep me naked all the time," he countered, flashing a pointy-toothed grin.

"That what he did? Because the no-shirt, no-shoes, not-your-pants look isn't fashionable this season last I checked."

He stopped smiling.

"I stole those off a clothes line. As far as he was concerned, keeping myself dressed was just another of my jobs. There's this stupid idea that giving anything at all to your thralls undermines a blood-bond. It doesn't. Bonds would be pretty useless with a loophole that big." He stood up and walked toward me, a calculating sort of look on his face. "But you, Elias," he said, coming close enough that I could feel the heat of his skin, "are refreshingly lacking in superstition."

"And you've figured that out...how?" I asked.

"Well," he answered, counting on his fingers, "you told me your true name. You broke bread with me—"

"I gave you a beer."

"Grain grown by the hand of man. Counts as bread. You should know that, or someone's been lax in schooling you," he teased. "So name, and bread, and now clothes. Three powerfully meaningful artifacts."

"And then there's the part where I fell into bed with you with little to no provocation."

"Well yeah, that. Goblins are repugnant. You're unclean now."

Something ghosted up the back of my thigh. I startled, and it took me half a second to realize that it was the tip of his tail. Tarn flashed a knowing smile.

"We are going to eat dinner before we start that again," I said firmly, reaching around to remove it bodily as it kept flicking against my thighs. Tarn's eyes closed as I took hold of it, making sure to be careful. It was only educated guess that told me that his tail might be sensitive, but that guess had proved true to a very interesting degree. I gave the whole length of it a slow stroke with my fingertips, and he shivered.

"Yes, Master," he purred. I considered correcting him again, but decided not to bother.

Because I could definitely get used to be called Master if Tarn wanted it that way.

———— ◉ ————

TEN MINUTES SAW ELIAS and I at his kitchen table, eating microwaved Chinese food straight out of the little paper boxes. Unmitigated luxury, and I was damned well going to milk it for all it was worth.

"So how does that work, if nobody's supposed to give you anything?"

"Goblins will nick anything that's left unattended," I answered, looking down into my box of greasy fried rice. "It's pretty much a given that anything that was left out without express orders not to be touched was fair game. He was twitchy about that, too...but he kept me caged most of the time he didn't want me doing anything."

"Caged?" Elias said, swallowing hard and reaching for his glass and looking at me with unhidden horror while he drank down whatever was stuck in his throat.

"Caged. Like, in a dog kennel. Hypocritical bastard, hating on anything made by the hands of man and then buying a damned dog kennel from Walmart to stick me in, but it was a hell of a lot cheaper than anything he could have bought purpose-made at the goblin market and hey, it's still cold iron."

"He kept you...in a cage,"

This level of horror at a concept that simple was probably a really good sign for my future well being. Because Elias clearly hadn't considered that as an option. I sincerely hoped that I wasn't putting ideas in his head. "He allowed me books," I said bitterly, "but only because I'd have gone crazy without something to keep my mind occupied, and he knew it."

I wasn't even sure what I'd said or done that spurred reaction, but Elias put his food down and embraced me from behind. His chin rested on top of my head. The bulk and strength of him was encompassing, his sudden presence shoving everything else to the margins of my awareness.

"I'd let you go free, if I knew how to do that," Elias said.

My mind stilled like water. It was a pretty thing for him to say... and I believed him.

Breath left me in a long stuttering sigh as that realization hit home. I believed him. As simply as that. Stupid. Why should I? Why did I? But I did. He'd said he'd have me free and I knew, knew that he wasn't lying.

Maybe he had stolen my wits. Maybe I was one of the cleansed and didn't even know it. Because worse than knowing he wasn't lying, I knew that the answer that sprang most immediately to mind was genuine.

"I wouldn't want you to, Master."

He didn't say anything. I might have died from humiliation if he did, and I kind of hoped he sensed that. He was taking the food out of my hands, and he was spinning me around, and he was kissing me. I didn't want to think about the ramifications of what I'd just said.

He was my master.

I was his thrall.

That was a very good thing. Maybe it was only the nature of the bond magic that made me think that, the same thing that made me obey orders that were given to me, but it felt so damned right to call Elias Master.

He was kissing me so well, moving from my mouth to my jaw. My throat. My ear, and that felt impossibly good. He had to know what that did to me, because he attacked with precision and skill and...well damn, maybe this was how humans went about making their thralls mindless. Because the capacity for thought was definitely waning in the face of care and comfort and blinding pleasure. Handed over freely, like it was nothing.

He picked me up again and carried me to the bedroom, laid me on the bed and pressed me down into it. I lost myself in him. In his humanity. When his hand found me I was desperately hard, and his hand was hot and calloused and enormous and so incredibly perfect as it stroked me. He tilted his head to whisper into my ear,

"I want you to fuck me."

My mind came to a startling halt, my eyes flying open in shock.

"You want..."

"I want you," he repeated, playfully, "to fuck me." He drew back, looking down at me, pinning me in place with those damned perfect green eyes of his. "Unless you don't want to," he amended.

"I..." I started, mouth dry. He'd taken his hands off me now, and that was good because it was so hard to think anything at all when he was touching me. "I haven't done that in...I don't even know how long."

"It's alright if you don't want to."

"I might not be any good at it."

"Practice makes perfect."

I couldn't help but smile at that. He leaned in and kissed me again, wrapping his arms around me and rolling so that I was on top of him. His face was flush when he broke the kiss, looking up at me playfully.

"What if I told you that you could do anything you want with me?"

"Anything I want?" I echoed, sitting back to look at him, straddling his midsection. I could feel his cock against my tail, hot and hard. I half-consciously brought the tip of my tail back around to toy with it. My tail having a mind of its own had its advantages...sometimes it knew what I wanted better than I did.

He said something softly, and I recognized it for an incantation before I felt the electric crackle of magic as it flowed through him, under his skin. Something was in his hand that hadn't been in his hand a moment before.

"Lube," he said with a smirk.

"Handy, you mages are," I replied.

"Aiming to please," he said, opening the tube and squeezing some into his hand. He slicked it over me in a hot, wet, firm glide and my mind went gloriously blank. He sat up a little, leaning back on his elbow. It made me shift downward, sitting on his thighs, and I didn't know if it was intentional on his part but when he shifted a little more his cock came bobbing up between my legs to lay flush against my own. He was so much bigger than me. Should have made me feel humble...but here he was outright telling me to do whatever I wanted with him. I moved to climb off his thighs, and he very obligingly spread them.

I kept my gaze on his face as I positioned myself and pressed forward, but I couldn't keep my eyes from slipping shut of their own volition as the intense heat and pressure and utter perfection of his body became too much. My world narrowed itself down to the meeting point of flesh pressing into flesh with a fluid slickness. As if it was meant to. I had to stop and be still and breath for a long moment when I'd pressed myself to the hilt, or I was going to come then and there.

I started moving. Elias groaned lowly, head pressing back into the bedclothes, dark hair fanning around him. His throat fluttered as he swallowed. He panted, hands fisting in the sheets as I held him by the hips and took him.

It was too perfect to think about.

Elias was made of life and magic and heat. The skin of his thighs was smooth over muscles that were iron-hard. A man made of power. My Master, who held me in thrall with all the power of blood magic.

And I was taking him.

I braced myself with one hand against the taut muscles of his belly and ran the other along the vast length of his cock from root to crown, palming the head. His eyes flashed open, green, piercing. I held his gaze as I thrust, and his eyes closed again. Stroke. Thrust. Stroke. Thrust.

More mind-shatteringly perfect than anything that had come before; I'd lived a thousand years and never had I known the likes of this. I brought my tail around and wrapped it around the base of his cock and squeezed. He moaned, and gasped, and came. The pressure was intense, almost painful, as I was held within him while his body spasmed in ecstasy. It broke me, and I came too.

As I pulled back from him and surged forward to lie against his chest, the thundering of his heart under my ear, it came to me again that he owned me. This was going to be my life now. He was going to hold me here, in this place. Hold me to pleasure like this.

This was the man that I was bound to.

His arms came up to embrace me, to hold me down against the quieting power of his body.

"I do believe this is going to work out fine," he said, his voice moving through me right to my bones.

"Yes," I replied. "I do believe it is. Master."

The Corporation Loves You

Forty-five times. She'd heard the message forty-five times in the last hour.

"Your call is important to us, please stay on the com. Remember, The Corporation loves you. Your call is very important to us, please stay on the com..."

The Corporation didn't know shit about Magdalena Pierrot, and if they did they would not have loved her. But that was all academic right now since she was dead in the water, out of fuel with less than two weeks of life support reserves left, and had been listening to this goddamned chirpy hold music for three goddamned days. Every few minutes the music was cut in with the cheerful monotone of the recording assuring her that her call would be answered by the next available associate. If Magpie got out of this alive, she was making it her personal mission in life to find the satellite that was transmitting to her coordinates right now and smashing it so hard it opened a quantum singularity.

"Here at The Corporation we strive to serve the needs of our faithful customers. You call will be answered in the order it was received by the next available associate. Remember, The Corporation loves you. Make yourself at home with The Corporation. Your call is important to us, please stay on the com."

Like she had any choice but to stay on the com. She'd sent out her distress call on a band she'd figured was secure and that satellite had picked it up anyhow and hijacked her com without her say so. Worse, it'd frozen her poor baby solid. She couldn't even turn down the volume unless she wanted to go hardware on its ass and start cutting wires—and though it was a royal bitch have to listen to elevator music and corporate platitudes, she wasn't quite ready to hack and slash her way to dying in a silent tin can in the middle of an asteroid field.

"... Remember, The Corpora—ATTENTION. APPROACH-ING VESSEL. ATTENTION. APPROACHING VESSEL."

Magpie's eyes went wide and she dived for the com. Emergency Override had kicked in, and she was able for the first time in three days to flip on the view screen. She hit 'mute' while she was at it. No more elevator music. When the screen flicked on, all the air went out of her like she'd been punched in the gut. The ship approaching had a Corporation logo plastered across its hull. That was the last goddamned thing Magpie needed, not when she had a hold full of jacked goods, weapons, and medical supplies intended for delivery into the hands of the United Freedom Alliance. They were supposed to have met her here a week ago. They were supposed to have brought her a new tank of xenon for the ion drive.

They were dead.

She'd suspected it for a while, but no doubt about it now. Most rebel ships were pasted together from salvage and duct tape and pretty damned near impossible to sneak past a security checkpoint. The Corporation didn't take well to anything they didn't manufacture. Had a habit of 'reprocessing available resources to maximum efficiency'—which meant melting down anything they decided was salvage in-to component parts. Including people who weren't loyal customers.

Magpie set her teeth and picked up her sidearm. She was a check-runner. Her ship was a gutted Corporation Freighter that still pinged as Corporate Subsidy, and most of the time she was damned good at pass-ing for legit. Most of the time she wasn't caught with her pants down in a place that nobody had any damned business being, though. This was probably going to get messy.

———◉———

FISH DECIDED TO CHECK out the distress call because it was the first unplanned thing that had ever happened to him. He'd been processing asteroids for ten years and he'd never come upon another vessel out here—there wasn't anything this far out except asteroids and more asteroids. Even process ships like his were spread thin and in rigidly ordered patterns that ensured they didn't cover the same ground. That would be inefficient. It wasn't a process ship that he was approaching. It looked like a G3 Freighter with some post-consumer modifications. There was something just a little off about it, and he couldn't place what. Aside from it being out here at all—that alone was strange.

It didn't respond to com contact. There might not even be anyone alive inside; he'd picked up the distress signal three days ago from an auto-response beacon. He sidled up to it and established an airlock connection without trouble. Pressure was higher on that side by a notch or two, and when the airlock equalized it sent some air from that ship hissing through the vents and it smelled—good? Unfamiliar. Something about it triggered a sudden pang in his gut, something out of the deep well of programmed memory. Something from a life he never had. Vat memories could be unsettling like that. When the hatch popped open there was a Typhon-class anti-personnel plasma rifle pointed at his face. He stopped moving. He could hear both of them breathing in the silence that followed.

It was a woman behind the gun. She was youngish, more than twenty but probably less than thirty. Younger than him... or at least younger than his body. Not really fair to compare ages with real people, since he'd spent his first years of existence in a tank with a cranial feed programming need to know information into his head. Enhanced Service Personnel hatched from the tank at twenty years' growth.

"You're too old to be a helmet head," she said, breaking the silence. There was something steely in her eyes; appraisal, maybe. "And you sure as hell are not Customer Service. Class?" she barked. Something inside him melted just a little, because she sounded exactly like a commanding officer. Part of his mind sang at having someone barking clean, crisp orders. It was a damned long time since he'd been worth enough of anyone's attention to get personal instructions.

"Resource acquisitions and processing, ma'am," Fish replied. "Only representation of The Corporation you're likely to find out this far, ma'am. Responding to your Customer Service Inquiry, ma'am. Here to help."

"Number?"

"99FF33F15H." He found himself inclined to look straight ahead into some imaginary distance. To avoid her eyes. Because she sounded like a commander, and insubordination was not tolerated. But her next question had his gaze snapping back, his heart quickening just a bit.

"Got a name?"

"Fish," he said softly. "Back when I had a unit, they called me Fish."

She snorted, a tiny smile playing out more in her eyes than on her lips.

"Magpie," she said. An image flashed through his mind of a black and white bird. He'd never actually seen a bird. Hadn't ever been dirtside. More vat memory.

"Magpie?"

"It's my name. Magdalena Pierrot. Magpie. You got buddies in there?"

"No, ma'am. Just some process bots."

"Do you get grid this far out? From your com, I mean? Can you ping to central?"

"No ma'am. I report back to central from Station Epsilon Delta once every fourteen days. My ship returns to central for load management, maintenance, and upgrades every six months."

"How long until they expect to hear from you?"

"Ten days, ma'am." Her gaze flickered up and down him, quick as a panel lighting up.

"Then unless you do something really stupid, I don't have to shoot you yet," she said after a pause, letting the muzzle of the gun drop just a bit. "Now back your ass up, I'm boarding you."

He did as he was told without really thinking about it, a sudden pang of anxiety flashing through him. He wasn't ready for an inspection. Not that this was one, exactly. At least he didn't think it was one. She hadn't identified herself to him by anything but name yet, and it would certainly be insubordinate to walk over to the com and plug her name into the database.

"So you're all by your lonesome in a ship this big, digging asteroids for six months at a time before you hit dry land?" she asked, catching his attention back. She was still oriented toward him, the gun generally trained on his position.

"That's right ma'am," he answered awkwardly.

"Pretty shit job, eh? You have emergency stocks? I need xenon, my tank's tapped out. Got in a firefight with some persistent disaffected non-consumers. Tried to contact Central, but we're too far out. I'm on my way to Epsy too."

She'd been directly engaged with disaffected non-consumers. That meant company loyalty. She might even be military or paramilitary division. A customer loss-prevention assurance agent out here hunting rebels. That would make sense; her presence in the asteroid field, her post-market ship to attract rebel attention, her possession of anti-personnel weaponry and extreme predilection for utilizing it to maximum efficiency. Shit. She was exactly the kind of person who'd happily report any and all aberrations to central. Fish was aberrant.

"I can assist you with that, ma'am," he said carefully. "I'll need your Customer Satisfaction Assurance number, or, if applicable, your rank and personnel number." The rifle came up with jarring speed, and she was standing there with gritted teeth and flashing eyes, looking right into him in a way that made his breath stop.

"All you need to know about me, 99FF33F15H, is that I am the woman with the gun and that I will shoot you dead if you seem like you're going to be a problem. My activities are classified. I trust that you, as an Enhanced Service Person if I'm not mistaken, are able to maintain intra-department information security? Because if you're not I'm authorized to terminate you."

"I'm here to assist you, ma'am." Fish said with more conviction than he felt, wondering just who or what she was. Why he'd gotten himself into this kind of trouble by coming to check out a distress call at all instead of simply reporting it to central. Customer assistance was not part of his employment profile.

"Show me where you keep your reserves," she ordered. He nodded curtly, keeping his eyes down as he led her through the ship. That meant leading her through the areas he'd modified. Modification of Corporation vessels was frowned upon. She stopped exactly where he'd hoped she wouldn't, and stared.

<hr />

THERE WAS A MURAL PAINTED on the adjoining bulkhead between the airlock bay and the body of the ship. Magpie looked at it, and looked back at the Corporation Drone, and then back at it. She took a step back to try and see the whole thing better, making sure to keep her sidearm ready. It was all made of these tiny, tiny little lines and hash marks in patches no bigger than her hand, overlapping each other and crossing each other, and no two patches seemed to be exactly the same color. They were all pretty close; variations on red and brown, arranged in something that suggested it should have a pattern but which she just couldn't piece out.

"That's different," she said. He was looking at the ground, looking damned nervous. "Application of alternate surface treatments for bulkheads and deckheads is covered in section 22a of the systems manual under maintenance and repair—"

"Where'd you get the paint?" she interrupted, looking back at him again. Couldn't quite decide what model he was—there were about a dozen kinds of Enhanced Service Personnel clones and she knew most of them on sight. But she'd never seen one that'd lasted this long. He looked about forty. Going gray at the temples. Most Enhanced Service Personnel burned out or screwed up or showed aberration or something by the time they hit thirty and were liquidated for resource reacquisition. He looked up at her, meeting her eyes. His eyes were that unnerving shade of grayish-greenish-brown that all clones had. He'd gone from nervous to plainly terrified. He hadn't looked scared like this when she had a rifle trained at his face, but now she was asking about paint and he looked like was about to piss himself.

"The alternate surface treatments have been manufactured from mineral powders collected in the cleaning and routine maintenance of mineral processing robots combined with spent engine cleaner. It seemed a most efficient use of refuse materials in the absence of requisitioned goods."

"You made paint from asteroid dust and shop slime? And you put it on your wall?"

"Yes ma'am. I understand that this may constitute and unauthorized modification—"

"Why?"

He swallowed thickly, eyes slipping sideways, to the room they were headed toward.

"It was a means of utilizing available man-hours during mission-crucial robotically-enhanced task management downtime. Ma'am."

"So you painted because you were bored."

He closed his eyes, apparently defeated.

"Yes ma'am."

"With paint that you made, by hand, by yourself, without any consumer goods."

"Yes ma'am."

"What was your department before you were reassigned to re-source acquisitions and processing?"

"Hands-on Special Operations Customer Care and Information Retrieval Personnel." She blinked, looking him up and down again. Looking at his face, the line of his jaw. He hadn't shaved in probably a couple of days. That was probably a dress code violation right there, but...yeah. Take ten years off the Drone and stick his face behind a shatter-resistant laminate sheet and she'd have been looking at Number Four Ground Soldier. Helmet head. Corporation shock troops for everything from quelling riots to running labor camps. He'd been one of those.

Which made it just plain weird that he was standing there now looking at her like he was scared. She'd never seen a helmet head look scared. Look much of anything, really—Ground Soldiers hatched out of the vat shark-eyed and jackbooted and ready to kill on command. The man standing before her wasn't anything like that.

"What was the precipitating event of your cross-departmental reas-signment?"

"Excellence of service resulting in retention of services beyond planned resource recovery operations. Special Operations personnel are retained for ten fiscal years. Upon review it was determined that my service record was sufficient to qualify for retention in a less intensive department."

"Followed orders good enough that it was worth more to keep you on, huh? Fair enough. I always wondered where they got solitary mining overseers from. Hadn't figured it was recycled soldiers though. Aren't the odds for aberration and degradation of mission-crucial em-ployee behavior patterns a lot higher than if they just minted a new batch? I imagine there's a high degree of loss in acquisitions this far out. Rebels. Mining accidents. Extrasolar phenomenon. One good EMP or Gamma Ray Burst and you're done out here. We've both seen just how much service provision is put toward attending customer service inquiries originating from these coordinates." She took a step nearer to him, and he leaned back a little. "Maybe they just expected you to die. I guess every bit of utility they can get out of you past your expected shelf life is just pure profit, huh?"

"It's been the prerogative of The Corporation that I not be liquidated. My Service Record is spotless, ma'am."

"Except you paint."

He met her eyes again. Stopped breathing. Swallowed. There was something really quite compelling about watching him swallow. About having his complete and undivided attention. Something very interesting, in fact, about looking at a piece of Corporation equipment that was behaving outside of expected parameters.

"You're aberrant, Fish. If this activity was reported to central you'd be liquidated."

"Yes ma'am. I would," he replied evenly.

"After ten years of doing their most mind-numbing work out here on your lonesome. Cleaning and keeping tabs on mining bots. Doesn't it ever bother you, Fish? Being all alone?"

"This is a solitary post, ma'am."

"Not what I asked."

"Employee satisfaction is not a measured parameter in the execution of this employment opportunity, ma'am."

"But I asked." She was close enough that she could feel his breath on her face.

"I love The Corporation, ma'am," he said, breathless, words tumbling out with tight perfection. "I trust that it makes decisions with the best interests of the people at heart. The Corporation loves me. I am at home with the Corporation."

"The Corporation doesn't love you," she said, closing the bare gap between them and laying her hand against his breastbone to feel the furious hammering of his heart. He gasped, eyes widening at the treasonous audacity of her statement. She leaned in and kissed him.

REALITY CAME APART at the edges for Fish the moment Magpie leaned in and touched her lips to his own. Impossible. This couldn't be happening because this didn't happen because this was not a thing that happened during the employment cycles of Enhanced Service Personnel. This kind of behavior was grounds for immediate termination without review. There was no way they wouldn't be found out; someone would review the security footage of the two of them entering this hallway and not coming out of it for too damned long and they'd put two and two together and both of them would be terminated on grounds of conflict of interest with mission-crucial employee behaviors.

But her lips were so soft.

Any and all negative feedback expressed about The Corporation was grounds for immediate termination, she had to know that.

But the hand that was willfully pressed against his breastbone slid downward, around the small of his back, and that sizzled along his nerves. His hands came to alight on her shoulders without any real effort on his part. She purred against his mouth; a soft, primal sound. A hungry sound. A sound that send vibrations through his suddenly hyper-sensitive lips and was perfect in a way that nothing this incomprehensibly wrong should be. When his lips parted her tongue darted inside, running slick and hot against his own. He felt himself reeling, falling backward against the bulkhead behind him and sliding down it to land, hard, on his ass. Found himself with his face inches from her crotch and Corporation keep him he could smell her through the fabric of her ship-suit. His gaze followed the line of her zipper from groin to belly to breasts to collarbone to throat and finally to meet her eyes and she gazed down at him in a distinctly predatory fashion.

"Show me your bunk, soldier," she said with her commanding officer's voice.

"Ma'am..."

"That wasn't a question, Fish. It was an order."

She reached down and took his hand and pulled him back to his feet. He looked away from her, not quite able to catch his breath. Still felt her eyes on him as he followed the order he was given and led her down the hallway.

"There's a camera there," he warned.

"They watch you sleep?" she asked, sounding vaguely disgusted.

"The Corporation's careful monitoring and recording ensures quality of service—"

"Spare me the copy, Fish," she interrupted. "If I wanted— oh... oh wow."

If he'd know that his vessel was going to be inspected he'd have gone to the painstaking trouble of removing all the evidence of his aberrant activities. Washing the paintings from the bulkheads, hiding the carved figures, recycling the tools he'd used. He destroyed them every six months just before his inspection, but it was four months since his last inspection and he'd amassed an admittedly large collection of them. He knew the camera's blind spots well, better than he should have. She was staring into the corner where his collection was painstakingly gathered, mouth slightly open, eyes wide in obvious appreciation... and he felt that unfamiliar tug of something again at the back of his mind. One of those emotions from the well of memory that he usually quelled instantly because it was wrong for him to think it. Pride, maybe. Probably. It felt really good that she was impressed by something he'd done. She turned back to him, and her dark eyes were smoldering.

SHE'D THOUGHT THE PAINTING was shocking. The sculptures were so much more than that.

They were abstract, like the mural had been, none of them a whole lot bigger than palm sized. Small enough to be pocketed, she guessed.

Asymmetrical stars, balls of little meticulously carved spikes, exacting-ly-wrought cubes scribed over with maze patterns, individually-carved chevrons arranged into a zig-zag grid that snaked along the floor. Pol-ished chunks of asteroids that seemed to be distillations of their origi-nal form. Oh, Fish had been busy. Busy because he'd been bored, and he'd gone ahead and done something about it. In defiance of his pro-gramming. In defiance of his mission statement. In defiance of every-thing The Corporation expected of its employees.

Fish was more aberrant than he knew. Probably didn't even under-stand what his work might represent. But Magpie saw it for what it was in all its thrilling, heart-stopping glory. Fish was evidence that all the bastards had to do was stop paying attention for a moment and the whole goddamned system would slip through their fingers. These were the seeds of glorious revolution, right here in the furtive three-di-mensional doodles of an understimulated clone left alone for a while to think.

What couldn't Magpie do with that?

She spun on her heel, her breath coming quick and heavy at the recognition of the potential before her. Looked at the reality of a clone left alone so long that it had somehow gained a glimmer of humanity. A man wiry from regimented exercise and short rations, face lined with concentration and survival beyond all expectations. Looking back at her like she was a goddess, all terror and awe, waiting to see what she would do. Waiting to see what she wanted from him. Waiting for his commands.

"Unsuit," she said, suddenly.

"Ma'am..."

"Unsuit, soldier," she repeated, talking a step toward him. She shrugged her sidearm off and let it fall to the floor behind her. He looked down, and swallowed thickly, and reached for his zipper. Teeth parted one by one with agonizing slowness, revealing skin with the markless quality that spoke of never seeing sunlight. He shrugged out of the suit, closing his eyes. Breath shallow.

And he might be terrified of her, but damned if he didn't find this just as sexy as she did. Couldn't lie about an erection that solid. There was exactly one thing more treasonous in the eyes of The Corporation than unsanctioned creativity. It'd been quite a while since Magpie had had a chance to exercise such gratuitous liberties, and certainly never with an Enhanced Service Person. With Corporate Property. She took the final step forward, close enough that they mingled breath, that she could feel the heat rising from his body and mingling with her own.

"Now mine," she ordered.

———⦿———

THEY NEVER MADE IT to his bunk. She caught him around the waist and pulled him into another searing kiss—this time in full view of the camera. They were both dead. But then, he hadn't ever really been alive. With her tongue sliding its way into his mouth and her hand gripping almost painfully at the back of his neck and her other hand sliding downward to his ass to pull him forward and flush against the heated length of her body, he was very certainly alive right now. His cock pressed against the smooth softness of her belly was unlike anything he'd ever even imagined.

"On your back on the floor," she ordered, her voice tight and low, almost a growl. He complied instantly, and she moved to straddle him, raised up on her knees. She looked at him, then lifted her head and looked directly into the camera.

"The Corporation will fall," she said. And before he could protest, before he could even properly consider the abject wrongness of those words, she sank down onto him and drew his cock up into the slick heat of her body.

Fish died.

Or at least he felt, in the moment of perfect stillness that followed, that everything that he'd ever known had ended and that the reality he found himself in now was wholly different than any he'd ever known. With Magpie poised above him, face still turned toward the camera, eyes closed, lips just slightly parted. Barely breathing.

Then she moved. The slightest rocking of her hips, face swinging down to gaze at him with eyes as dark and deep as the view out a port. She laid her hands on his shoulders, fingertips caressing the place where his throat met his collarbone, and she rocked again. And again. And again. A slow, even rhythm that he understood in the cores of all his bones. Animal instinct, even underneath his programming, below the vat memory. This was right. This was life. He found his hips jerking up in time with her rocking, following the heat of her body, slick and smooth and wet and fluid and impossibly beautiful. He came, harder than he'd ever come in his life. It was nothing like the quiet, empty relief he sometimes brought himself in the hygiene bay. It was staggering and liquid and blisteringly hot, and he was sure that it would kill him. This was a star going nova, all energy consumed in a moment of brilliance beyond comprehension. He groaned with the intensity of it, and the groan became a sob which gave way to panting as she smiled down at him. She collapsed against him, head on his breast, both of them slick with the sweat of such effort.

"See, Fish?" she purred, and he felt the vibration of her voice in his breastbone, "That's what you can expect when you defy The Corporation."

"They'll review the footage in ten days. We're going to be terminated."

"You think I'm gonna leave the footage lying around for them to find?" she asked playfully, rolling off him and folding her arms behind her head. "It's easy to break a camera, Fish. Definitely gonna keep the footage from that one though," she said, pointing to the camera directly behind them. "For future viewing."

"The cameras are tamper-evident..." he faltered, wondering at his sudden inability to panic. At the languorous calm and delicious exhaustion that had taken root in his mind and body in the wake of what she'd done to him.

"And I don't give a damn if they notice that the cameras have been tampered with. See, Fish... guess you haven't caught on yet that I am neither an associate of The Corporation nor a loyal customer. I live off the grid."

He flashed a glance at her, trying to be scandalized as he should have been. Trying to correct himself as he should have done. But he couldn't feel anything but joy and awe and sudden, aberrant, blasphemous, unshakable loyalty when he looked at her.

"I'm a pirate," She said with a feral grin. "And you're loot."

"You intend to appropriate Corporation resources and materials?" he asked.

"I sure as hell do. I do believe I'm going to sack this ship down to the rivets and panels. I could do with a couple of mining bots, some fresh supplies—" she ran a single finger down his breastbone and belly and traced a quick circle around his navel. "—an Enhanced Service Person of my very own."

"An aberrant one, you realize?"

"I wouldn't have it any other way," she said with a feral grin. "Now kiss me already."

And Fish was more than happy to do as he was told.

The Flower of Innsmouth

In the autumn of 1865, I was commissioned by Captain Obadiah Marsh, the great patriarch of Innsmouth, to produce portraits of his family—a matter of some delicacy, I came to understand. The Marsh clan was extensive, Captain Marsh having several children from two marriages and the eldest of those children already married with children of their own. There was an oddness about the family, though one not entirely uncharming in most cases. Still, the two youngest sons of the Marsh family had faces of—well, perhaps it was kindest to call it character. In any case, it required an artist of great skill and greater prudence to depict them in a flattering light. But the daughter...

Octavia Marsh was, in my opinion at least, a vision of most perfect loveliness.

She was narrow-faced, with an upturned button nose, enormous liquid blue eyes, and corn-silk hair; but it was Octavia Marsh's mouth that had first entranced me. It was wider than could be considered strictly pretty, I supposed, but with lips so lush and pouting that watching her speak had driven me half to distraction upon our first meeting. Her mouth seemed entirely too fleshy, too wanton and wicked in and of itself, to belong to such a dainty young blossom of a girl.

She'd become twenty in the summer before the autumn when we met, the youngest product of Captain Marsh's second union. She was sharp-eyed, ever keenly regarding everything around her with unblinking directness and the earnestness of a scholar. While the other family members tended toward dour silence while they stood to be painted, Octavia chatted with me amiably and laughed easily. Not the twittering songbird laughter one might expect, but a true cachinnating that revealed a depth of mirth and wisdom uncommon in a woman so young.

She was fluent in French and Latin, I learned, and more than passingly good with several other ancient languages—a most erudite scholar, trained in Europe at no small expense. The Marsh family at large were antiquarians, as was apparent in the appointment of their home. Their library was rich with absolutely ancient tomes, many of them under glass for the sake of preservation. The overall sense of the Marsh home was one of stately refinement; Innsmouth was a golden port, newly rich by the efforts of men like Obadiah Marsh. He'd opened a gold refinery on funds acquired in youthful sailing ventures to the South Seas, and had in his possession a great many lovely and enigmatic artifacts hailing from the same.

It wasn't fortune that mattered to me, though. Octavia Marsh could have been a pauper's daughter and I'd still have courted her.

I declared my intentions to her father shortly before I'd completed the last of the family portraits, and he gave me his blessing in a disconcertingly perfunctory manner. Perhaps it was only that he was eager to see her happily wed; he was not a young man by any means, and she was his last child. It caused me no little anxiety how closed-mouthed and furtive her family seemed at large, but Octavia assured me that it was only their way. There were few outsiders who deigned to visit Innsmouth—there had, in fact, been frank discussions in her youth as to which of her cousins would be most suitable for her to marry, should it come to that. The Gilmans, the Waites, and the Eliots were all interrelated in complicated ways and, among the four families, one could find the better part of the seaport's population. They were, then, quite glad to have a bit of new blood.

The matter of religion seemed to be the worst of it.

Innsmouth was a superstitious little town, and I came to learn that all four of the great families—and thus the overwhelming majority of the townsfolk—subscribed to something of a local cult. It reminded me of nothing so much as the sort of skullduggery that college fraternities and Masons and those sorts of people got up to. Octavia was uncharacteristically quiet about it, and this I took for mild embarrassment at her family's unorthodox manner. She absolutely did not wish for me to visit Innsmouth at all upon Halloween, and instead rather forcefully insisted that she and I would be attending a gathering elsewhere. I deferred to her concerns and spoke little of it, and we spent the evening at a lovely party in Boston with some school friends of mine. Octavia got on swimmingly with my friends' wives.

The truth of it was that I was utterly enchanted with Octavia and would have deferred to anything at all that she asked of me. My friends, of course, were terribly amused by this, joshing me about falling for some country girl who'd never even seen Boston before, but my parents were quite pleased that I'd met a girl from a family of some quality. Mother had lost all hope for me when I'd declared plans to dedicate my life to art.

The winter of 1870 was a congenial one, spent in cheerful correspondence from her home in Innsmouth to my own in Arkham, and by springtime it was not at all uncommon to find either of us staying for days at a time with the other's family.

So it was that I was staying at the Marsh home when the storm came to Innsmouth.

It was one of those frightful springtime storms that can happen so suddenly upon New England shores in April, with thunder and snow at once, and the sort of winds that can shake even a steadfast old manor to its foundations. The sort of night best served by a cheery fire and mulled wine and good company—all of which we had in abundance.

Only, as the night wore on, every member of the Marsh household artfully excused themselves from the drawing room. At half past nine, when Captain Marsh declared that he was going to retire, I realized with a shock that Octavia and I had been left entirely unchaperoned.

"Octavia, I do believe we're alone!" I said with some mild concern as I watched her casually drain her cup and smile at me over its edge.

"Oh, are we?" she mused, glancing around. "I suppose we are. Shall I show you to bed then?"

She regarded me with eyes as deep and liquid as any ocean, and my mouth suddenly went a bit dry. I don't recall answering in the affirmative, only that she took me by the hand and walked with me up the grand staircase into the tenebrous winding hallways above, her movements perfect in their fluid poise. Octavia floated like an angel, her feet making not a sound, the hem of her skirt never rising above the carpet. It wasn't the guest room that she led me to, but her own.

"Octavia..." I began, but she laid a finger across my lips to silence me, and I felt a sudden thrilling tightness in my belly.

"Won't you come and sit with me a while?" she offered, meeting my eyes with her usual unblinking directness.

I never had been able to nay-say her.

She led me into her bedroom and closed the door behind us and spun on her heel to kiss me. It wasn't our first kiss—that I'd stolen on the Halloween night we'd shared in Boston—but it was by far the most bold and wholly indecent. It left my knees weak and my head reeling and my breath short. That ample mouth moved over mine. I opened my eyes to find that she'd never closed hers, their marine depths peering into me as if she could plumb the depths of my soul.

She broke our kiss, pulling bare inches away so that when she spoke, I felt her breath against lips made acutely sensitive.

"Won't you stay the night with me?"

"Your father..."

"I'm certainly not thinking of Father just now. You shouldn't be either."

She glided across the room and turned down the gas lamps, leaving the room in a murky dimness that very nearly hid her. I saw her in silhouette as she moved toward me, my mouth dry and my heart pounding at the absolute impropriety of this. At the thrilling, impossible, wanton, forbidden, carnal, and unimaginable turn the evening had taken. I'd never so much as seen Octavia's unclothed ankle, never laid a hand upon her thigh for more than the barest moment before she demurely removed it. She had always been most perfectly modest and coy. In the echoing distance, thunder rolled, and another volley of sleet pelted the windows with a smooth hiss. Lightning flashed, and I saw it reflect in her eyes with a ravenous light.

"I want a springtime wedding," she whispered, taking me by the hand. She led me to her bed. She bade me sit upon it. "But I don't think I'll wait for it. I'm not like other girls," she whispered into my ear. It was the last warning I had before Octavia straddled me, and I found her words to be more true than I ever could have imagined.

I might have cried out in shock had she not captured my mouth with her own, muffling my cry as she moved upon me with a strength her slender form belied.

Octavia Marsh was not hiding the shapely legs I'd so often envisioned beneath those voluminous petticoats. I knew more than a little about the anatomy of the fairer sex, from art and from... baser texts. What met and quickly consumed my legs was an alien mass of seething flesh, a dozen or more writhing columns of sinuous muscle, twining around my calves, my thighs, encircling my waist with inconceivable, boneless power. I moved to push her away, and she caught my hands in her own, twining her fingers with mine, pushing me backward until I was lying against her bed, my feet dangling helplessly over its edge, her mouth never leaving my own.

The kiss, when she finally broke it, left me gasping.

"There's nothing to be afraid of, darling," she said. Even as she spoke, one of those slithering limbs moved around my waist, the tip of it as dexterous as any shapely fingertip, deftly slithering its way beneath the waistband of my trousers. It found the hem of my shirt and slipped beneath it. The muscles of my abdomen contracted upon its contact—it was warm and smooth and just the slightest bit slick.

Laughter bubbled out of me then, quite against my volition, and it had the sound of madness in it.

She released my wrists, but I found myself quite unable to move, paralyzed in shock, in terror, in a curiosity as dark and unfathomable as any that has ever come upon man.

Octavia began unbuttoning my shirt.

Octavia's hands were large, outsized for her otherwise poised and dainty frame. I most deeply appreciated that fact and its ramifications as they ran with electrifying boldness across my flesh as it was bared. I drew a gasping breath, my body reacting with an impetus not quite my own, my hands moving with shuddering trepidation toward her slender waist.

She purred.

It was a dark noise, bestial and primal, and it seemed to rumble through me with greater strength than the thunder that echoed it.

The writhing mass of tangled limbs atop me moved in concert to unfasten my trousers.

I realized, with dull surprise, that I was as hard as I had ever been.

I dared a glance downward, beneath the hem of Octavia's skirt, to find everything below my navel lost in an untraceable knot of tangled, shining flesh, writhing curves of alien composition that defied all reason. My vision swam, and I looked away, looked upward, to find the lovely and impossible form of Octavia's shoulders, her sculpted arms, the curve of her throat. She unfastened her hair and tossed her head with girlish delight, whisper-light curls the color of seafoam in the darkness tumbling free to cascade about her face, her eyes never blinking.

She unbuttoned her dress. Even as I watched, she shrugged it off, baring a pale shoulder, letting the bodice fall downward into the tangled and unknowable mass. Behind her in the darkness, liquid shadows moved with all the studied poise of a pair of hooded cobras, and it took me long moment to realize that I was watching her make calculated use of her tentacled appendages to deftly unlace her corset. I rose up upon my elbows, as much liberty as her position would allow me, my eyes straining in the darkness as the garment fell away. Her skin shone, almost shimmered, in the glimmering light of the gas lamps. So pale that the light cast off it in an ephemeral, scintillating blue, like the inside of an oyster's shell.

The limbs twined about my own moved with a hideous knowledge, caressing, tips insistent and curious as they peeled my trousers away and let them fall to pool around my ankles. They were so very warm and numerous, sliding across flesh that no other living soul had ever touched, arousing an impossible lust within me. I closed my eyes against the onslaught, moved to near madness as they slowly coaxed my thighs apart. One of them wrapped soundly around the base of my manhood and gripped it, sliding like a serpent until the whole of it was captured, the tip of it moving across the crown of me, spreading the pearl of wetness it found there.

I am not ashamed to admit that I moaned then, as guttural and animal a noise as may come from a man. Her tentacles were swarming all over me now, caressing my arms and legs and chest, one of them moving with studied care across my face. When it traced my lips and insistently pressed between them, I couldn't help but accept it. It tasted of salt, of the musk of womanly flesh. I wrapped my lips around it and suckled.

Octavia surged forward, hands on my shoulders, my hands on—well they couldn't properly be called hips, I supposed. She positioned herself with care, and I only understood what she meant to do a bare moment before she did it.

She sank down upon me, drawing my manhood into the center of that writhing mass, into a tight, hot, wet passage that was quite unlike anything I could have expected. It was not formed as a human woman should be; there was no maidenhead to breach. In that moment, God preserve me, I did not care. The tentacle in my mouth probed so deeply that I choked upon it, and it recoiled with a speed that had me gasping, coughing, drawing breath in great panting heaves that shook us both.

Something hot and slick probed between my buttocks in insistent exploration. I think I made a noise of protest then, and certainly tensed at the intrusion, but Octavia chose that moment to tighten her nether muscles in a paroxysm around my manhood, as if she meant to draw it up into her body entirely and the whole of me with it.

She grabbed my wrist and pulled my hand up onto her breast, squeezing, instructing me of what was wanted. When I dared follow that instruction, cupping and squeezing in gentle exploration, that narrow, slick tip breached me.

Another peal of mad laughter passed my lips as I realized that I was being buggered by Octavia Marsh even as I fucked her.

And then the tip of that probing tentacle touched something within me that made my guts tighten and my vision sparkle with stars for a moment in a pleasure beyond bearing. I might have reached my climax there and then had Octavia not crushed her mouth against my own, biting at my lip with such force that I worried for a moment that she would draw blood.

She writhed, and I bucked, and together we moved in a carnal dance of squirming, thrashing, writhing flesh. She moved within me, and I within her, as we fucked one another with abandon.

There was a clap of thunder, and a bare instant later a flash of lightning that illuminated the room. In stark relief I saw Octavia, the statuesque perfection of her breasts, the soft curve of her belly, the writhing, slithering mass of slickly shining tentacles that enfolded me in a state of unwholesome pleasure.

"Ia! Ia! Cthulhu fhtagn! Ph'nglui mglw'nafh!" she cried, her voice sonorous and consuming. "Cthulhu R'lyeh wgah-nagl fhtaga!"

She spasmed around me, the mass of tentacles tightening at once, gripping every inch of my body with tight heat so that I couldn't so much as take a breath. Her nether depths stroked me within, wet and hot and wild and unknowable, moving as nothing human should move.

I came with more brilliance than any man has ever known.

I say this with absolute conviction.

She collapsed upon me, panting, her breath hot upon my throat, her mass of tentacles slowly releasing their various grips, sliding warmly over my skin as they arranged themselves in what I supposed was their most usual order.

She discarded her dress and came to lie beside me in her naked glory, and I leaned upon my elbow again to look upon her in the near darkness. She was aware of my scrutiny. I didn't doubt that. But she met my eyes with a direct, unblinking gaze that halted any words or questions I might have had.

To the waist she was a woman, as perfect and lovely as any ever captured in art or spoken of in song. Below, she was a tangled mass of slick and shining tentacles, some alien creature beyond all reason that I knew man was never meant to know. Even as I watched, those slithering limbs—of which there must have been a dozen, at least—pulsed gently with a muscular power that had my mind scrambling, reason and truth screaming at me as I looked upon the monstrous, seething form of Octavia Marsh, with whom I had just shared a carnal embrace.

We were married in June of that year.

Jackrabbit

The day after I turned eighteen, I went and got a tattoo of the three hares on my belly. It was a motif that had shown up everywhere from Chinese folk art to Islamic reliquaries in Russia to Cathedrals in Germany to craft guilds in southern England. I'd been kind of obsessed with Gothic architecture in high school, and also a dabbling Wiccan. My mom had thrown a blue fit about it, which at the time had been a major plus.

Ten years on, I was working as a design consultant for some low-end production company and making decent money selling commissions online and wondering what I was even doing with my life. I just hadn't hit my lucky break; didn't have the money for proper art school, didn't have the connections for loftier things than office work. My paintings had never been displayed at a show I hadn't paid to be in. My high school self would not be pleased to learn that a couple of years shy of thirty, I was sitting in a crap room in a chain hotel in Kansas.

It was supposed to have been a three day conference. I was now on day four, because inclement weather was keeping flights down. It was the first week of March, and back home we were getting those horrid springtime storms with thunder and snow. At least the weather was nice here.... Since I was stuck in middle of nowhere, Kansas, for another 24 hours with a company rental car and nothing particular to do, I decided to poke around a little. Which was how I found the store.

It was in the same plaza as a Whole Foods, and it was called 'Earth's Heartbeat.' I'd walked in at first just because it smelled amazing, and once I was inside it felt rude to leave without poking around a little. It was one of those new-agey book stores that catered to spiritual types. The proprietor was a little old man with long gray hair and a neatly-trimmed beard and horn-rimmed glasses. He watched me with this sort of grandfatherly welcome from the moment I stepped inside.

"You're not from around here," he said with a wry smile. "New in town?"

"Nah, just here for a conference. Passing through."

"Well then, how lucky I am to have made your acquaintance at all," he said, bowing his head a little bit. "R.J. Fox, at your service, and welcome to Earth's Heartbeat. Let me know if you have any questions about anything you like. Did you come in looking for anything in particular?"

"No, thank you. Just looking around," I answered with a smile.

So I kept poking around, mostly just to take in the smell. It was incense and essential oils, overlaid with the assorted scents of dried herbs and paper and leather and dust. One wall was all books on assorted witchy topics, the top shelf containing used books that might warrant a closer look. The opposite wall was herbs in great big jars, arranged alphabetically. In the middle of the store were a couple of free-standing tables and shelves cluttered with all kinds of things; crystals and singing bowls and silver daggers and golden chalices and scented candles and handmade soap.

When I saw a wooden box with the three hares inlaid on its surface, I had to open it.

The box was lined in blue velvet, and there was a rabbit's foot inside. It was nothing like the standard keychain ones you could get at dollar stores. It was a dusty brown color, paler on the bottom of the foot, instead of the usual garishly-dyed rainbow assortment. It seemed longer and skinnier than a rabbit foot should have been, and it had claws—really obvious visible ones, as prominent as a dog's claws. It had a sharp bend at the back, the little pewter finial that covered the cut end sitting at ninety degrees to the bottom of the foot. The pewter was stamped with an image of a rabbit's face, looking straight at the viewer, and there was something about its eyes...something far too knowing.

"Ah, now that's a rare thing you've put your hand on," the old man said, unfolding from his chair like a spider. "That's the left hind foot of a hare, with all its ankle bones intact, from a hare that was snared in a cemetery on the night of a full moon that happened on Friday the thirteenth, and it was cut from the animal while it still lived. I believe this one dates from 1984. The setting's older, of course. Civil War era, if I'm not mistaken."

"How much?" I heard myself asking before I could think better on it.

"Oh it's not a thing you can just buy, I'm afraid," the old man said with a coy smile. "You can only get it if you're lucky. Follow me."

I stood there with my feet planted as he crossed the store and pulled back a curtain behind the register, turning to look at me expectantly. I still had the box in my hands.

"You want it, you're going to have to come with me. Otherwise you can put it down. Wouldn't hold it against you, if you don't think your luck's good enough."

I glanced down at the box again and felt a strange little flutter in my belly.

Well, why the hell not? Guy looked like he weighed about a hundred pounds and might break a hip if he took a wrong step; it wasn't likely that he was planning on jumping me. I followed him into the back room.

The back room smelled like pine resin and smoke and animal hides. Sitting in the middle of it, right under the light from the single bare light bulb that the old man turned on by pulling a chain, was a wheel. Like a wheel-of-fortune kind of wheel, with about a hundred little slivers on it with various little symbols on them.

I glanced at the old man. He just looked at me and nodded to the wheel.

So I gave it a spin.

It went around with a mechanical clatter, the silver pointer running almost musically along the pins that divided the slivers, a blur at first but then slowing so that I could see individual images flashing by. The grim reaper. A woman with a sword. A black cat. A snake poised to strike. A crow. A naked man.

It landed on a sliver with an icon of the three hares in white on a black field.

I felt a tightening in my belly, right under the tattoo, and the old man whistled.

"Well, looks like we have a winner," he said with a sly smile. "Been waiting on someone with the right kind of luck for twenty-odd years, you know."

"So I can buy it?" I asked, still feeling a little shocked, unable to look away from the symbol on the wheel.

"No, ma'am," he said. "You can have it."

I was finally able to tear my eyes away from the wheel and look down at the box in my hand. It felt heavier than it ought to have; had it been that heavy a moment ago?

"Hope it serves you well. If I were you, I'd go down to Nicky's Pub. There's a fella there who'll want to shake your hand. He's been saying he's got to buy a pint for whoever wins that little piece of luck for years. You show him a pretty young thing like you won it, he's likely to buy a whole round in your honor."

So that night, after stopping back at my hotel to freshen up, I did.

Nicky's Pub was one of those little bars that was clearly by and for locals and had probably been around as long as the town itself. There was an antique rifle mounted above the bar, and photos of winners of 'Monthly Trivia Madness' on the wall along with newspaper clippings about local high school sports teams. I got second glances just walking in, so I made a bee line for the bartender.

"The old man at Earth's Heartbeat sent me here," I said, reaching into my bag and pulling the box out, "because apparently there's someone here who wants to know that I won this."

The bartender looked at it, and his eyes widened. He looked at me, and back at the box, then he grinned and laughed aloud and shouted across the room,

"Hey Jack! You'll never believe who just walked in!"

At one of the tables in the back, a man stood up and began sauntering over.

He was a skinny guy, maybe thirty or so, and he had legs from here to Easter Sunday. His skin was light brown and sun-kissed, his face narrow but his nose and mouth wide for it. He had sandy brown hair, big brown eyes, and a curious smile on his face. There was a small shiny scar, the barest hint of indentation, running from his lip up to his nose. I wouldn't even have noticed it except that the light caught it just so.

"This lady here won old man Fox's wheel of fortune game," the bartender said behind me.

"Really now?" he asked, looking at me in open appraisal. I felt my cheeks flush a little, because guys didn't often look at me like that. I was alright, when I made an effort, but I wasn't anything special.

"To whom do I have the pleasure of speaking?" I asked.

"Name on my driver's license is John Leveret, but ain't nobody in this town who doesn't call me Jack. And you, pretty lady?"

He had that kind of Midwestern drawl to his voice that made me think of cowboys and horses and wide open spaces. It'd be lying to say it didn't make me melt a little bit.

"Selene," I answered softly.

"Ah, like the moon," he said, grinning properly. His front teeth were kind of prominent. Not enough to really call buck teeth, and not enough to make him look silly, but definitely... something. Another detail that just made his face that much more compelling. "You're not from around here are you, Selene?"

"No, I'm not. Just passing through. My flight's supposed to be to-morrow afternoon."

"Well then, I guess we don't have very long to get to know one an-other," he said with a smile that was downright suggestive. "But if you really won that little treasure off Old Man Fox—"

I held the box up and flipped it open with my thumbs. He looked at the rabbit's foot and then looked up to meet my eyes, and I felt my belly tighten. Those were hungry eyes.

"—Well I'm just going to have to buy you a drink." he finished, still looking at me. "In fact, what the hell," he turned to look at the bar tender and shouted, "Round on me! To Selene, the luckiest woman this county's seen in twenty-three years!"

A cheer went up through the bar. Jack ordered a beer, so I ordered one too. He invited me back to his table to chat.

He learned that I was an artist. I learned that he was a trucker. He learned that I was from Maryland but currently lived in New York. I learned that he was 'local, but liked to range.' Someone pumped a cou-ple of quarters into the neglected jukebox in the corner, and a Carrie Underwood song came on.

"You wanna dance?" I asked, offering my hand. He didn't take it. He just looked ruefully downward.

"I don't dance so well, actually," he said, rolling up the leg of his pants. From the middle of his shin on down, he had a shaft of steel in-stead of a leg. I could see the top of a plastic foot in his shoe. "I'm sorry," I said, feeling a little bit flustered. "I didn't mean—"

He laughed, low and genuine, rolling his pant leg back down and shaking his head.

"Nah, don't you worry about it, just hope it doesn't put you off too badly."

"What happened?" I asked.

"Patch of bad luck when I was just a young thing, not even two years old. It's not worth talking about. Doesn't trouble me too much, except I don't dance."

So we just talked, and ate—I learned, to my great surprise, that he was a vegetarian—and he had another beer while I sipped soda because I had to drive. Round about midnight, he asked where I was staying. I offered to show him.

My hotel was about half an hour from the bar, and he spent the entire car ride there whispering absolutely filthy things in my ear while I tried to keep my eyes studiously on the road.

He had me pressed against the back of the door the second I got him inside the room, taking my mouth in a consuming kiss that shot fire down my spine and straight to my groin. He pulled back, leaving me gasping, and I stretched my arms over my head and arched my back as his hands found my ribs and moved along them to cup and massage my breasts. He kissed his way along my jaw and down my throat, his hands moving down again and then up the back of my shirt.

"I don't usually do this kind of thing—" I gasped, letting him lift it up over my head.

"Then I'll just consider it my lucky day," he said, stepping back and slowly unbuttoning his own shirt before peeling out of it...and then he stopped.

He was looking at my tattoo, his eyes fixed with sudden, rapt attention.

"Well, would you look at that," he said quietly, running his finger around the edge of it, tracing the path that the hares were running. I swear, just having him do that had me weak in the knees, and I put my hands on his shoulders to steady myself. He was all lean muscle, and when I pulled him back against me, I learned that the sparse hair on his chest was softer than I'd have imagined it. I found myself running my fingers through it, feeling the jackhammer beat of his heart. He slid his hands down my back and under my ass and hoisted me up. My arms went around his shoulders and my legs around his waist automatically as I was lifted, and he spun me around and carried me to the bed, letting me fall back against it. He stopped here, standing at the edge of the bed between my knees, looking into my eyes for a moment before his gaze went lower, fixing again on my tattoo. Like it meant something. I might have said something about that, except he looked at me again and smiled then dropped to his knees and traced it with his tongue. I moaned, pushing my head back against the bed, and in one fluid move he undid my pants and hooked his thumbs into the waistband of my panties and shoved the lot down around my ankles. He moved southward from my belly and devoured me.

"Oh God," I moaned, sitting up enough to plant my hands on his head to keep him right where he was, and finding that his hair was impossibly soft. It was my last focused thought before I completely lost my mind to the work of his tongue. I dug my heels into the small of his back, curled over him in helpless bliss, hanging there in a moment I never wanted to end.

"You didn't strike me as a church girl, Selene," he said, muffled by my thighs, his breath hot against my most sensitive flesh. I groaned, and he moved up my body, kissing his way along my belly and my breasts, sucking at one of my nipples while he undid his pants. He met my eyes for a moment before he put himself inside me.

His rhythm was slow at first, but got harder and faster in a building crescendo, never faltering. I drew my knees up more, stretching my legs so they rested right on his shoulders, and he straightened up some and the angle was absolutely perfect. He turned his face a little to kiss my ankle, meeting my eyes as he did, and it was all over for me. I came, hard and brilliant, curling my hands into the sheets and howling at the ceiling. He thrust a couple more times, but then he was shuddering, gripping my ankles hard and going still, sweat-slick and shining under the fluorescent light and so god damned beautiful.

He lay down next to me on the bed, panting, and I turned just a little to curl against him.

"Well, that was something," he said languidly, once he'd caught his breath.

"It most certainly was," I replied with a silly grin. He crawled up onto the bed properly, and I moved to lie next to him. I fit against his side like I belonged there, falling into instant comfort against him, listening to the drumming of his heart. Seemed faster than it ought to have been, somehow, but deep and even and comforting. I closed my eyes, listening to it.

I opened them again to the sound of running water and found myself alone in the bed. The glowing red numbers on the clock told me it was four in the morning, pale moonlight casting beams across the floor that led a silvery path to the bathroom. There was light coming out under the door.

I entered the bathroom quietly, and Jack didn't seem to notice me, too concerned with the particulars of washing that gorgeous sandy-golden hair of his. The water cascaded over the taut muscles of his back, running in long rivulets over the delicious curve of his ass, down lean thighs and long calves to pool and ripple and drain away below. I found myself transfixed, standing there in the doorway watching him, but finally my reverie was interrupted when Jack asked, mischievously, "Care to join me?"

"I do believe I will," I replied, breathless, stepping forward without hesitation.

Jack met me with a hot, wet embrace, the water cascading over me as he pulled me into the spray. I bit my lip, wondering what I'd done to please fate so.

Jack's hands were all over me, as if he meant to memorize every inch of me. He spun me around and held me from behind, drawing soap-slick hands along my ribs, cupping my breasts and sliding his thumbs across my nipples before moving down again. He drew teasingly light fingers across my belly, halting frustratingly short as he nipped at the back of my neck. I tentatively reached a hand up and tangled it in Jack's wet hair, wondering at the softness of it. Jack purred approval against my neck, fingertips making their way down to my cleft and teasing the flesh they found there. Not entirely ready for that, I turned around and dropped to my knees.

Jack was a very well-put-together man. I'd certainly enjoyed that before when he was fucking me, but getting a decent eyeful of him was something special. I ran the flat of my hand up the length of his cock from root to tip, listening to his breath hitch. I leaned in to nuzzle him, taking in wet heat from the shower and the unmistakable scent of lust. He stopped breathing altogether for a long moment when I took him in my mouth, and then he made a long, pleased purring sound. I licked and sucked and teased, getting lost in the taste of him, and when I was sure that I was just shy of driving him over the edge, I kissed his crown and stood up. He leaned forward, and I felt his length nestling itself against my ass.

I closed my eyes and just basked in the pleasure of those teasing fingers while Jack's other arm held tight around my waist. He moved against me in tight little thrusts, nipping at the back of my neck again, caressing the flesh with lips and tongue and teeth.

"Get inside me already," I groaned, leaning forward, bracing my hands against the shower wall.

He didn't wait for a second invitation. I felt his cock, hot and hard and deliciously huge, pressing its way into me. God, it had never been like this. It was pure and unconditional bliss, and I lost myself in it, pressing my forehead against my hands, my hands against the tile while Jack fucked me senseless. He was like a machine, his rhythm perfect, going faster and faster until I had no choice but to scream out my climax against the shower wall.

Clean and sated, we collapsed back into the bed again.

"I didn't even think about condoms," I said, comprehension dawning on me in those last lucid moments before sleep came. "I mean, I'm on the pill and everything, but—"

"Don't you worry yours about it," he said into my ear. "You're a lucky woman, Selene." He put a hand on my belly, right over my tattoo, and it felt warmer than it ought to have. Warmer than it made sense to be, and I could feel the warmth seeping into me. "And ever shall you be from this day on."

I nodded, tucking in against the length of his body. His hand stayed there, warm on my belly, as I drifted off to sleep.

I woke up to my cell phone's alarm telling me that it was time to start pulling myself together if I wanted to get to the airport in a timely fashion. There was no sign of Jack, but I hadn't really expected there to be. I'd expected to feel hollow and empty about that, or cheap, because I was not the kind of girl who engaged in one-night-stands with truckers... but it didn't feel like that. It felt like something really important had happened. Like something in my life had changed.

I showered and packed, slipping the box with the lucky rabbit foot inside into my luggage. Coffee in one hand and handle of my rolling suitcase in the other, I meandered across the parking lot trying to remember what my rental car looked like and where I'd put it, when movement caught my eye.

There was a jackrabbit running in the field across the street. It was leaping and rebounding and running in crazy circles, like it was just showing off. I stopped to look at it, and in the middle of one great leap, it seemed to see me, stopping still when it landed and looking right at me. It had the same knowing eyes of the rabbit stamped in pewter. After a long moment regarding me, it dashed away into a patch of scrub that separated the hotel from the highway.

Waiting for my flight, I checked my email to find one marked 'urgent' from one of my friends at the co-op studio where I painted when I got the chance. Some guy from a local gallery had stopped in to see one of the other artists and noticed my latest work in progress and was practically demanding to see more of my work! My heart was pounding as I heard the boarding call, and in my belly I felt an echo of that same strange warmth I'd felt last night when Jack had put his hand over my tattoo.

It wasn't until I got all the way home and unpacked that I learned that the lovely wooden box I'd gotten from Mister Fox was empty. Where the rabbit's foot was would forever be a mystery.

A month and a half later, I learned that, while I might have lost my rabbit foot, I had brought something back from Kansas. I'd been on the pill, and it had been the wrong time of the month anyway, but from what I knew about the fabled hare from my time as a dabbling Wiccan... well there were always ways around such details.

My son was born with a harelip, but they can fix that sort of thing easily enough these days.

I named him Lucky.

Omega

T hat's the problem with time travel into the future. You go to the past and get your ass stranded, you can always leave messages for your future self. You stray too far into the future, on the other hand—well, thousands of people go missing every day. It's a known fact. Sometimes people just vanish.

I met her at a Circuit City in western Massachusetts. I'd just walked away from being asked for the third time if I worked there, because a chick in a polo shirt and slacks just has to be an employee even if her shirt's the wrong color. She was trying to buy a chronoton sink for a self-stabilizing resistance engine. Gotta give the sales girl credit, she hadn't called security yet.

"It's 2006," I said, walking up behind her. I forget why I was there. I think I was looking for cooling fans or something. She had the kind of hair you only see in shampoo ads; bouncy and curly and halfway down her back, black that reflected blue under the fluorescent lights.

"Yeah, I'd gotten that far," she said without turning around.

"Chronology stabilizers weren't mass marketed until the 50's," I said.

"Son of a bitch," she groaned, throwing her head back.

"We could hit up Home Depot for some tinplate and magnets. I've got a truck."

She turned and looked at me, and I saw that there was an iridescent tattoo near the corner of her eye. A butterfly. She looked me up and down appraisingly. I gave her a passing glance. Tank top. Straight jeans. Ballet flats. Pretty good time-neutral outfit for anything from the late 1970's to the 2050's or so.

"Oh, so you're just gonna build a chronoton sink by hand?"

"Yeah," I replied, raising an eyebrow. "It's not that hard."

"What're you, a mechanic?"

"Not formally, but I know my way around a class-three engine," I replied, scratching the back of my neck. She was a model or something. Had to be. She snorted a little, a smile tugging at the corner of her mouth.

"Yeah, ok," she said. "I'm Tina."

"Eden," I replied.

"Well ain't you just," she said with a slow smile.

I wanted to keep her.

Eden. Her name was Eden. She had no idea how hot she was, and that was part of what made her hot. I was so damned tired of over-confident party girls who thought they deserved a medal for just show-ing up. Of girls who were just like me. Girls who were me, because Aphrodite clones came a dime a dozen. Tired of glamor and glitter and genetically engineered pheromones oozing out of every pore. I wasn't supposed to ever get tired of those things, but I was defective. Aphrodite clones were supposed to burn out after five years or so in a supernova of fast life and dissipation or something like that. Most of us OD'd by my age.

Eden was pure. An untouched human. She hadn't told me as much, but it wasn't the kind of thing that I had to be told. They didn't make girls like her where I was from, not anymore. She had freckles, for fuck's sake. Genuine ones. And pert little tits, and the most luscious ass ever. Wasn't any reason I couldn't keep her, if I played my cards right.

She didn't even know that I was a clone.

"So confession time," I said, running my tongue along my teeth, "I kinda sorta don't have any real currency that works for herenow. I've been working from this wallet some guy left at my place..."

She gave me this look of perfect scandal, stopping dead in her tracks. I grinned at her.

"Wouldn't be telling you if I didn't feel a little bad about it, Sug-artits. Was gonna ask if you mind springing for burgers is all. I haven't eaten all day."

"You plan on looking for the guy to give him his wallet back?" she asked suspiciously.

"Cross my heart I would, if I knew how. I've got this whole 'fish outta water' thing going on." I let her catch up to me and slung an arm around her shoulder. "You're the first person I've met who's willing to be my Temporal Native Guide."

She snorted a little, shaking her head.

"I'm not even a little bit native to herewhen. Hometime's the 3010's. I restore junk time machines—there's a hardware bust going on herenow. Circuit City's circling the drain, with a bunch of other store-front companies; you can pick up retro hardware really cheap. I've got about fifty bucks of local currency, if that means anything to you. Pawn-shop swap. Guess I could spring for lunch."

I grinned widely, pulling her in closer. She tensed up a little, but she didn't try to squirm away or anything. Better and better.

"There's this little burger joint on the corner a block from here. I think it's cheap. Lemme show you."

The burgers were awesome. She agreed that the prices were good. I trusted her judgment on that, since she seemed to have a pretty good grasp of local economy what with buying and selling parts or whatever.

"So what are you doing herenow?" Eden asked, picking at the salad she'd ordered to go with her burger, not really looking at me. Delight-fully shy. "I mean, forgive me for assuming, but you don't seem to have come prepared or done the research."

"Got stranded. I was shooting for 1960's USA with intent to hit the nomadic music festival scene for a while. I've got wardrobe and everything. It's about as far back as I've ever been on Earth. I'm not re-ally into archive-crawling or anything. You?"

"I pop back sometimes, for touristy stuff, but there's so much red tape if you want to go back past the industrial boom that it's just not worth the expense. At least not for me."

She sucked her soda down to the bottom, and it made a guttural sound.

"You like to party?" I asked laconically, looking at my nails.

"I'm not any good at it," she answered with a shrug. "I'm a big dork. All the better for tinkering with machines freelance. All my best friends are engine parts."

I couldn't help myself. I reached across the table and ran my hand playfully through her short, fluffy hair. It was blond right to the roots, and if she was only from the 10's it was probably that way without being genetically tinkered with.

"That's just a little bit tragic. You doin' anything for the rest of the afternoon? Or, hell, the rest of this week herenow?"

"Not really..." she answered noncommittally, narrowing her eyes at me.

Turned out it was a good thing I didn't have anyplace to be that afternoon, because after lunch and Home Depot we went to her ship and after we were inside her ship we lost track of time. In both a figurative and a literal sense. Her place, just now, was parked in an empty lot between an abandoned convenience store and an apartment building with a giant Units Available sign.

Her ship was huge. Not on the outside; it just looked like a late-model truck camper on the outside, but there had to be a thousand square feet of interior, with a kitchen and a bathroom and everything. Total rat's nest of stuff, too. She told me to help myself to what was in the fridge. It was mostly Japanese soft drinks from the 1990's in either 'blue' or 'pink' flavor. I wanted to go through her software before I took a look at the engine. She was cool with that.

"You are NOT telling me that you've got a busted Omega drive," I said, leaning over the console and trying to work out how she'd organized her schematic files. If she had. It wouldn't have surprised me to learn they were all just stuck in random folders with random file names.

"You got a hearing problem, Sugartits?" Tina said, emerging from the underdeck panel, a smudge of grease on her forehead. She'd removed her shirt at some point while she was down there, and climbed up out of the floor in jeans slung low enough on her hips that she couldn't have been wearing anything beneath them. Her bra was red, and strapless, and a size too small. Analytical details were the kind of thing I noticed. She stretched her arms above her head, hips tilted, her neck and back making satisfying cracking sounds.

We'd been in her ship for three hours now, according to my watch. If she had a well and truly busted Omega drive, my watch might well just be jewelry at this point.

"If I didn't have a busted Omega drive, I wouldn't be looking for a chronoton sink now would I?" she said, staring at me, running her tongue along her teeth. That appraising look again, maybe with a hint of challenge.

"There's a lot of reasons..."

"You got a girlfriend?" she asked, cutting me off.

"No..."

She stalked up to me and grabbed the back of my head and pulled me into a brutal kiss, the bare skin of her belly and shoulder hot through the thin fabric of my shirt. The smell of fresh sweat and engine grease rose from her; my hand, seeking purchase, found the small of her back—bare skin on bare skin, hers slightly slick. She snaked a hand behind me and grabbed my ass and snapped her hips forward, all one fluid and obviously practiced motion.

I had no idea what the hell had prompted such a response on her part.

At that point I really didn't care either.

Stupid logic had to kick in about then and point out that this was not the kind of thing that happened to me. I was the mousy, nerdy, pear-shaped chick who refurbished classic time machines. I had either fucked up somewhere and made a dimensional transporter and landed my ass in the porno-verse after my jump this morning, or this was the part where she told me I was on live broadcast. I braced my hands against her shoulders and pushed her away. It was a whole lot harder than it really should have been. She took a step back and licked her lips and giggled.

"What the hell?" I demanded, feeling a little bit dizzy. My lips felt hot and tingly and almost bruised.

"Well, there's a couple of maybe reasons a chick like you doesn't have a girlfriend," she said with a wicked grin. "Just figured I'd rule a few of them out. Like you not being into girls."

"You could have asked."

"Where'd the fun be in that?"

"You're crazy."

"All the best people are. I'm gonna hop in the shower—I got engine grease in my hair."

She disappeared through the archway, unhooking her bra. I watched her go, eyebrows hedged together, glancing up at the corners of the room for hidden cameras. She reappeared a moment later, topless. She had utterly perfect breasts.

"That was an invitation, Sugartits."

Live broadcast or not, I wasn't waiting for her to ask a third time.

I followed her into the bathroom. The shower was already running. The bathroom was small enough that the spray got my shirt wet.

"You oughta take that off, it's gonna be soaked in a second." she said, casually peeling out of her jeans. I'd been right—she wasn't wearing anything underneath them. I was suddenly horrifically self-conscious about my cotton briefs. Sexy underwear was the kind of thing girls like her sprung for. I bought mine by the ten-pack. I tried to slide them down along with my slacks so she wouldn't see them and got my pants tangled up around my ankles and lost my balance. I tripped, falling into the full spray of the shower with my shirt still on. I'd probably have cracked my head open if I hadn't literally fallen onto her, face planted right into those perfect breasts of hers. She laughed, and it shook both of us.

"You need to calm down, sweetie," she said, running a hand up the back of my now sopping-wet shirt. The fabric clung and pulled and bunched around her wrist as her hand snaked up and unhooked my bra with practiced efficiency. She managed to help me stand up and start pulling my shirt up over my head all in one fluid process. She tossed it, along with my bra, out of the shower. It hit the wall and then the floor with a wet thud. I really hoped she had a dryer someplace in this flat or I was gonna be stuck here way longer than I'd planned on.

And then she locked her eyes on mine, and my mouth went dry. Because she was looking at me like she was planning to do dirty, dirty things to me. Like nobody who looked like her ever looked at anybody who looked like me. What the hell alternate reality had I stepped into?

"Whenwhereall are you from, sweetie, that you can built a chronoton sink from spare parts and still wiggle like a Puritan girl just from unsuiting, hmm?" she asked, her voice gone soft and slightly smoky.

"Kappa Kappa Prime in the 3010's, originally," I confessed, looking down at the space between her feet and mine. Her toenails were painted bright purple, stark contrast to the coffee-and-milk color of her skin. Starker contrast than the fish-belly pale of my own feet.

"I thought Kappa Kappa was supposed to be the spire of heaven. Good Kappa girls don't grow up to be dykes."

"Yeah, well, I don't live on Kappa Kappa anymore, do I?" I replied, setting my jaw and looking back up at her. If she was teasing me I was gonna leave her ass here to rot even if I had to walk out in sopping wet clothes.

But she smiled then, slow and predatory and hotter than she had any damned right to be. She leaned in close to whisper in my ear, her voice dropped down so low that I had to strain to hear her over the shower.

"So I guess you've never been to Earth in the 3050's then, Sugartits? Because you sure do seem to have missed the fact that I'm a model six Aphrodite clone." She closed the bare inches between us, the whole slick and hot and gloriously naked length of her pressed against me, and licked her way along the shell of my ear.

"But that's really refreshing, you know?" she said playfully. "Means you didn't come back to my place because you expected me to be an overclocked super-slut." Her hand ran down the length of my back, cupping my ass. "Not that I'm not one, mind you."

"This cannot be real," I whined, letting my head fall back.

"Real is relative, sweetie," she said with another giggle. "I was grown in a vat. So maybe that makes me less real. But I pegged you right off as the bitch who can give me what I need, today."

She slipped the hand that wasn't grabbing my ass between us, moving downward with narrow and frightfully nimble fingers along my belly and into my curls and deftly right into the cleft there. When the tip of her finger touched exactly what she was looking for, homing in like she had a fucking GPS locked on, I moaned long and low with all the breath I had in my body. My arms went around her without my deciding to do that.

"There you go, sugar," she purred. "This is as real as you can make it."

My breath came back in a gasp, a sob, as I closed my eyes and held on and let her do whatever the hell she wanted with me. Because what she wanted to do with me was hotter and more intense and more impossible than anything that anyone had ever done. Her lips were on my neck, little nibbling kisses moving down along my throat, along my collarbone. Two fingers down, along the slick flesh between my legs, fingertips pushing inside and thumb pressed up on the slick, tight nub of flesh and rubbing. The hand on my ass slid upward and backward, along my side and along my arm, grabbing my hand and pulling it to her breast. Her hand over my hand, squeezing just a little. Giving me directions. I was more than ready to take whatever directions she wanted to give.

She rubbed her face against my breast and made a pleased little humming noise. Opened her mouth and licked, closed her mouth again over one nipple and sucked. I shuddered, resisting the urge to push her away because it felt like too damned much.

She bit my nipple.

I screamed when I came.

I pretty much collapsed against her, and she let me slide down the hot length of her so that I was on my knees and panting. I smelled sex. Realized I had my cheek laid up against her thigh and my panting breaths were making little droplets of water spray off the immaculately-groomed thatch of soft hair at the meeting her her thighs. I tilted my head back and looked up at her. She was looking down at me, fire in her eyes. The shower spraying over her back, making rivulets over her shoulders and down her breasts. Nipples taut and dark. Her hands on my shoulders.

"Well?" she asked. A challenge.

I licked up the length of her slit, closing my eyes. She was tart and slick and just the slightest bit salty, and she purred loud enough for the vibration to shake her her belly. I felt it. I liked it. She buried her fingers in my hair and held me there while I feasted on her. It had never been like this with anyone. I wasn't sexy enough for this kind of thing. But she was sexy enough for both of us. Her breath was coming in quick gasps, sharp little moans that sounded almost like pain. She dug her hands into my hair with enough force that I whimpered, and she made a long high animal noise, shuddering and holding me still.

And then she dropped to her knees and pulled me head back and kissed me again, grinding her whole body against me.

It was a while before I realized that the shower water had gone cold.

"I really need to get that generator looked at," she said against my neck. "Know a good mechanic?"

I threw her wet clothes in the dryer at her request. I came back to find her stationed in front of the console again, clicking through files. Wet. Naked. Not apparently concerned about either fact, but she blushed pretty when I came up behind her and wrapped an arm around her waist and laid my chin on her shoulder. I felt it, the heat that came rising to her skin at the impropriety of... me.

"Might be a while on those, Sugartits. Out of hot water means the electrics dodgy, and heating elements are the first things to go. Dryer's running cold."

"Figured that," she said, sounding a little short of breath. "Wanna watch TV for a while with me? I've got a whole wall console in my room."

"Yeah, ok," she answered. I'm pretty sure we both knew that we weren't watching TV.

We collapsed together onto the bed in front of the console. I turned on the screen, but neither of us were watching it. I started playing with her hair, going spiky in that stage between wet and dry.

"You're gonna turn it into a frizzy disaster," she said, pulling away a little and folding her arms behind her head. "So what was it you were saying about being a clone? I don't have any history past the 3020's. Futurology weirds me out."

"I'm an Aphrodite model six. It's a popular model. There's like half a dozen of us on the staff for every club back home, I swear. All party all the time. It gets old. I originally came to the US because clones have full amnesty here. Started history surfing because folks in my hometime only figure an Aphrodite's good for one thing." Eden blushed again, turning her head away. I took the opportunity to kiss her on the back of her neck, and she shivered a little. "I came to earth because home wasn't home anymore. Not for me or my girlfriend. Like you said, good Kappa girls don't grow up to be dykes. We hitchhiked to Earth together right on my eighteenth birthday. She dumped me like six months later for some chick in a band. I was working tech support at a time machine repair kiosk... I just kinda kept doing that. Got good at it. Went freelance.

Gonna be coming up on thirty this year, biologically speaking. I've only had a couple of serious girlfriends since. Haven't got laid at all in like a year and a half—"

I had to interrupt her, because angst was not the direction I'd had in mind. Didn't know what to say. I was a party clone. Hadn't ever had what could be called a girlfriend, not really.

So I just went with that I knew and rolled on top of her and pulled her into a kiss.

She melted. Put her arms around me and kissed me back like it was a prayer. Kappa Kappa heritage, maybe it was. Wasn't anybody prayed for clones. Made me feel special like I knew I wasn't. Like Eden was.

I kissed along her throat, and she tilted her head back and let me. Kissed along her collarbone, a long slow kiss on each nipple, little nipping kisses down her belly and down one thigh and then moving into the tart sweetness at her center. She gasped, and squirmed, and I had to push against her thighs because she kept trying to squeeze her knees together.

"Sorry... sorry... sorry..." she whimpered between gasps.

I looked up at her, over the plane of her body. "You want me to stop?"

"Oh God, no!" she hissed, eyes closed, lip swollen because she'd been biting it.

"You don't need to be sorry, Sugartits," I replied with a smile before tonguing her sweetly. I slipped one of my own hands between my legs, a fingertip on either side of my hotspot, just teasing myself. She was almost sobbing now, her hands dug into my sheets. I sucked on her clit, and ran my tongue along it at the same time.

"Jesus!" she shrieked, loud enough that people outside might have heard, if anyone happened to be out there.

"Close, Sugartits," I breathed, resting my head on her thigh as I finished myself off. "But my name—is—Tina!"

We lay together on her bed for a long time, and I couldn't remember the last time I'd felt so good. I was still waiting for the other shoe to drop. Tina was flipping through the channels, head in my lap, content as a purring cat. Like it was just normal.

"So you wanna go pick up dinner with me or something?" she said languidly. "I don't know what time it is outside, but there's always this place on the corner a couple of blocks from here, other direction from where we had lunch. It's a death location, so it swaps out every few years. It was pizza last time I checked."

"Thought you wanted me to look at your generator."

"Yeah, and I want you to look at my engine, too. And I want you to spend the night. I've got this whole agenda I'm working on, in case you hadn't noticed. Next on it is food."

"I haven't changed my assertion that you are crazy."

"And I haven't called you wrong, Sugartits."

"My name's Eden."

"Yeah, I know."

"Whenwhereall are you from, Tina Aphrodite, sexy clone?"

"The future-tur-tur-tur, obviously," she replied with a grin.

"Buenos Aires, originally, but I'm from the web so that's immaterial. Vat bitch—never was a kid or anything, but I already told you that. Got bored with the whole 'bouncy sex fiend' scene and decided to poke around looking for better. It's been fun. I'm kinda between jobs right now, ya know? And, uh, I've sorta been here, like here-here, since the 1960's. I wasn't quite lying when I said I was aiming for the nomad concert scene..."

"But?"

"But it's confession time again," she said with a sign, sobering a little. "I got stuck. Like in this spot. Because my Omega drive's a little bit fucked. Figured if I waited long enough, eventually I'd run into someone who knew what they were doing or at least a store'd open up that had good tech support."

"How long did it take you to get from the 1960's to now?" I asked, guardedly.

"I dunno, couple of months? It's been pretty boring, really. I only got web access last week."

"So that was what, the 1990's? Early 2000's?"

"That assumes we're going in order. I don't think we are."

She looked up at me, head still in my lap. Waiting for what I was gonna say to that, because she sure as hell had not told me that walking into her house meant I didn't know when I'd be walking out.

"I left my truck in 2006," I said, tightly.

"If I'd warned you that we were playing Rip Van Winkle in my apartment, you wouldn't have come in," she replied, and for the first time since I'd met her she looked just a little worried. "I liked my truck."

"I can buy you another one. If you can get me to 3050 Buenos Aires, I've got loads in the bank. The bouncy sex fiend scene pays good."

"Never been to the future. I've got nothing to wear," I said petulantly. "And I don't think your clothes are gonna fit me."

"You stay long enough to fix my drive, we can so work on that."

"We'd better."

She sat up and hugged me tight, and I sighed, trying to keep from smiling. She was completely unfooled, and rubbed her hand through my hair vigorously enough to generate spray.

"Sugartits, welcome to adventure."

About the Author

M onique Poirier is a time traveler from 1983, currently residing in Providence, Rhode Island. An enrolled member of the seaconke wampanoag tribe, she is a leading voice for Native Steampunk. Her stories have been featured in many Circlet Press anthologies, including the "best of" *Fantastic Erotica*. Her novel, *Cygenic*, is forthcoming.

If you enjoyed this book, you might also enjoy...

Superlative Speculative Erotica
edited by Cecilia Tan and Bethany Zaiatz
Twenty of the best erotic science fiction and fantasy stories published by Circlet Presson our 25th anniversary. A little cyberpunk, some high fantasy, a touch of horror, some superheroes, a bit of space opera, some paranormal... What unites these stories is their quality. The anthology also features characters who identify as lesbian, gay, genderqueer, bisexual, trans, and heterosexual. What label do you put on a book like that? We call it... superlative speculative erotica.

Fantastic Erotica
edited by Cecilia Tan & Bethany Zaiatz
To celebrate the 20th Anniversary of Circlet Press, Fantastic Erotica presents the very best erotic science fiction and fantasy short stories published by Circlet in the past five years. Chosen by popular vote by the readership from among all the stories published by Circlet from 2008 to the present, these favorites are the cream of the crop.

Best Fantastic Erotica
edited by Cecilia Tan
The best erotic science fiction and fantasy as determined by the annual contest run by Circlet Press. Rewarding originality and positive sensuality, the contest inspires well-known and unknown writers alike to excel in this provocative genre. Erotic sf/f combines erotic and sexual themes with magic, futurism, high fantasy, cyberpunk, space opera, magic realism, and all the many other sub-genres.

All Genres  All Genders

Circlet Press: Erotica For Geeks www.circlet.com